COWBOY RICHES

By

Herb Marlow

COWBOY RICHES

By
Herb Marlow

CHAPTER ONE

My eyes flipped open to darkness, my ears filled with the lost-soul moan of the wind curling around the eaves of the bunkhouse. I knew it was morning, but I sure hated to start the day. During the night, the blue norther that was stalled above the Red River moved south to add its misery to a cowboy's life. No news there and it sure wasn't the first time. People who worked in some warm store in town seemed like the lucky ones this morning, but I knew I'd never last at such a job. I'd tried it once, but it didn't work out, and even if I knew anything that would get me a job in town, I wouldn't stick with it. Horses and cattle were all I'd ever known; I reckoned cowboying would take me to my grave.

Mid-October was early for a blue norther in North Texas, but the cold wind didn't care. At the Slash T Ranch, we were facing the last day of the fall gather, and while the weather hadn't been exactly friendly the past week, it hadn't been this cold either. It would sure enough be bitter in the middle of a horse today.

Suddenly, the overhead lights flashed on, and a harsh voice called, "Up and at 'em! Let's go! Up and at 'em!" I rolled to a sitting position and reached out for my socks hanging on a boot top, automatically pulling them on. I stood and stuck my legs one at a time into the Wranglers draped over a chair, and then sat down again to stomp into my boots; the spurs attached making music at each stomp. I picked up a towel along with my shaving kit, and moved toward the bathroom. At least I knew the water would be hot for shaving. When it came to the important things, the Slash T took better care of their hands than

3

any ranch I'd ever worked for.

When I entered the dining room through the door from the cowboys' living room, I saw that the ranch hands were already there, eating pancakes and sausage. I nodded to one or two, sitting down by a young man named Tom. Tom Hansen was eighteen and employed as a ranch hand, but I knew he wanted to be a cowboy.

The ranch hands lived in their own area on the west side of the dining room and kitchen. I assumed it was identical to the cowboys', but I'd never been in it. Ranch hands were ranch hands; cowboys were cowboys. The ranch hands took care of the buildings, fed the horses and registered cattle kept near the buildings, and planted and harvested several thousand acres of wheat each year. They built and repaired fences, made hay and kept the machinery running. They were farmers, fencers, carpenters, plumbers, roofers and mechanics, but they were *not* cowboys.

The cowboys did the range work. They liked best to do their work from the saddle of a horse or the seat of a pickup, and they would quit in a heartbeat if told to do ranch hand work. It was up to the cowboys to take care of the range cattle, to work the cattle and ride the fences, to doctor and brand, to gather the range herds when needed, to sort and ship the cattle. Both ranch hands and cowboys were necessary on a spread the size of the Slash T. Set in the rough mesquite covered hills south of Childress, Texas, George Tomlinson's holdings spread over two hundred sections, 128,000 acres.

As I filled my coffee cup from the pot sitting on the table, and began to load a plate with fried eggs, bacon, hash brown potatoes and sausage, the cook, Handy Rowell, stuck his head out of the kitchen door and yelled, "Fresh eggs comin'!"

I grabbed two slices of brown toast from a heaped high plate and began to eat. "Gonna be cold out there today, Joe," the young ranch hand ventured.

I nodded my mouth full.

"I sure wouldn't want to be up on no bronc this mornin',"

Tom continued.

Chuckling, I said in a low voice, "That's why cowboys get paid the big bucks."

Tom laughed at that. I reckoned I was kind of Tom's hero because he always acted sort of flattered when I talked to him. Tom was a friendly kid, and I liked him, but I didn't think he would ever make a cowboy. For one thing, ranch hands rarely got the opportunity to do any real cowboy work that would give them experience. For another, Tom was a city boy, raised in a poor family in Wichita Falls, and he'd never seen a ranch until he was out of high school. Most cowboys were country boys who started learning cowboying skills when they were kids, never really thinking about being anything else.

My comment about "big bucks" was laughable. Cowboys made an astounding $900.00 a month plus found (food, lodging and horses furnished), ranch hands got the princely sum of $700.00. Neither group would ever get rich from their pay packets.

When the men finished eating and were all drinking final cups of Handy's good strong coffee, I called out, "Hey, Handy!"

The cook stuck his head around the kitchen door. "Whatcha want, Garth?"

"You goin' down to the South Pens to cook for us today?"

"Yep. The boss told me you weenies would have to have some of Mother Handy's chow or you wouldn't be able to stand the cold. 'Course, I'm drivin' down in my warm pickup truck, not riding a big fat horse like you big tough cowboys!" He cackled with his toothless mouth wide open.

"That's good, Mother Handy," I retorted. "And speaking of fat horses, make sure you skin the next one you feed us. This horse hide you call sausage is tougher than your hard-fried eggs."

The men all laughed, but Handy took his revenge. "Why, I'll do that, Joe. I figured to fry up your buckskin for dinner. You want a ham or a hock?"

With an outraged yell I sailed a piece of toast at the cook.

"You keep your meat cleaver away from my horse, you worth-less pot banger!" Laughter filled the room. Handy and I had been friends for several years. We met when both of us worked for the Spade Ranch down by Colorado City before we came to the Slash T, and our joshing gave the cowboys and ranch hands a lot of entertainment.

My buckskin wasn't a Slash T horse; he was my own geld-ing. Not all of the cowboys owned a personal horse, but I'd trained Buck when he was a three-year-old, and he was about the best horse I'd ever straddled. The ranch allowed the hands to keep one horse on the ranch, fed and penned at no charge. They didn't lose anything on Buck, though. He was a top roping horse, one I'd won money on at local rodeos, and while I didn't use the gelding for range work, Buck would be waiting for me at the South Pens where the cattle would be worked and sorted for shipment. That's where he'd earn his feed when I roped calf after calf, and he dragged them to the branding fires.

The foreman, Matt Walters, stuck his head in the door from outside and called, "Okay! Let's go!"

With groans and curses we shrugged into our gear and went out into the cold. I went to the large round pen where the horses were kept and slipped inside with my rope in my hand. Because all of the cowhands knew that I was the best roper on the ranch, I was the only one who entered the pen. The cowboys climbed the high fence, pointed at the horses they wanted from the milling herd, and my rope would snake out and drop over the head of the chosen mount. The rider would come in with a lead rope and toss my catch rope back to me. The cowboy would lead his horse out while I dropped a loop over the next horse's head.

I caught two horses for each rider, for they would have to change mounts at noon. The work we were going to do tired horses out in a hurry. The extra horses would be trailered to the Midway Pens where the cowboys would eat their noon meal. The horses in this pen were the ones we used every day, and we all knew which ones would stand the long cold miles the best.

Regardless of what the cook said, none of the horses were fat, but they were all in good shape. They were well-muscled quarter horses, born and raised on the ranch and trained for cow work.

Once the other cowboys were taken care of, I roped out my own mounts, a dark sorrel with a blaze down his face, and a rangy gray. The men who had been the first to get their horses were now mounting them to work the kinks out and warm them up a bit. Some of the horses tried to protest the cold morning by humping their backs and crow hopping, but the cowboys soon settled them.

I tied the sorrel, a known bucker, to the hitch rack in front of the saddle shed and went in to get my gear. Before leaving the shed I unzipped my heavy coat, pushing the headstall up under my arm, bit first. This was both for the horse's benefit and my own; putting a cold bit in a horse's mouth on a freezing morning was just asking for trouble. I zipped the coat back up, pulled my saddle off the rack along with the heavy saddle blanket, and pushed through the door back out into the cold. The north wind was brutally cold, blowing hard, almost parallel to the ground. Sleet and snow added to the wind made things even more miserable, stinging any exposed skin like buckshot.

I wiped the horse's back with my sleeve and swung the blanket into place with my left hand, following it with the saddle swung up with my right. The horse humped his back at the weight of the saddle, but I ignored that. I tossed the cinches over to the offside, reaching under to pull the front cinch up, threading the end of the latigo through the saddle ring, and then back down to the cinch, pulling it up and through one more time. I pulled the latigo tight, left the end dangling, and then reached under the horse and grabbed the flank cinch, threading it through the buckle and snugging it up.

Now came the bit. Standing on the left side of the horse, I pulled the headstall out of my coat and held it in front of the horse's head, my right arm over the poll between the ears. With my left hand I fed the bit into the sorrel's mouth, and the warm bit went in easily. I pulled the bridle over the horse's ears and buckled the straps. Finished, I unsnapped the lead rope and coiled it up to attach to the saddle on the left side of the pommel, picked up the reins, and began to lead the horse around in a large circle.

Since I was the last man to mount, the others were all watching me, shouting advice against the wind: "Walk him 'til he sweats, Garth. Then he won't buck!" "Hey, Joe! Want me to top him off for you? Wouldn't want you to get hurt in your old age when he throws you off."

When I stopped leading the sorrel around I moved to his left side, pulling the latigo tight and making my tie, and then followed that move by pulling the flank cinch tight. The horse was showing some white in the eye that looked back at me, so I grabbed the cheek strap of the headstall and pulled his head toward me, making him circle.

Now things had to happen quick. I let go of the headstall, grabbed the looped reins in my left hand, stabbed my left boot into the stirrup, grabbed the saddle horn with my right hand, and swung up, holding the sorrel's head high as I searched for the right stirrup. When I found it, I shoved my boot deep and let the reins go.

The horse bogged his head, pitching forward in a straight line. The other cowboys whooped, but the show didn't last long. I didn't want the sorrel to build up a sweat, not in weather like this, so I pulled his head up, danced him around in a circle until he settled, and then swung down. I loosened the cinches just a little, and led the horse to one of the trailers.

There were two long gooseneck stock trailers hitched to pickups standing nearby. Each trailer would carry four horses, two in the front compartment, and two in the rear. The idea was to drop the cowboys and their horses at intervals of two or three miles from east to west. I knew that I would be one of the first to start out, so I loaded the sorrel into the rear compartment of the nearest trailer, along side a brown horse that Fat Charley Bryce would be riding.

The pickups pulling the trailers were four-door Ford super cabs, easily holding five men, and more than that at a pinch. I climbed into the warmth of the pickup attached to the trailer the horses were in, knowing it would be the last time I'd be really warm until noon.

The pickups were driven by ranch hands that would drop the cowboys off, return to the headquarters for the remaining horses, and meet us at the Midway Pens for nooning.

Unfortunately, Bryce and I were not in the warm pickup for long. The truck followed a two-rut ranch road west along a low ridge, stopped at the first drop off point while Charlie and I climbed out. Once the horses were unloaded, the pickup moved on down the road. We tightened cinches, swung aboard and headed into the brush with our backs to the cold north wind.

The plan was for us cowboys to cover the area from the road to the Midway Pens, collecting cattle and driving them south. That sounded easy, but it wasn't. The cold north wind and stinging sleet would not let up, and the cattle would be holed up in warm spots, very reluctant to move out, though at least driving them south they would have the wind at their backs.

I was almost instantly cold right through the many layers of clothing. I was wearing cotton long johns next to my skin, covered by a flannel shirt and denim jeans. Over the shirt was an old MSU sweatshirt, though I had never attended that university, or any other for that matter. My coat was heavy, wool-lined denim with a high collar and a flap at the back that dropped down over my rear. Heavy leather shotgun chaps covered my Wranglers, and on my feet I wore wool socks inside my Tony Lama boots. My hands were covered with sheepskin lined hunters mittens. I'd tied a scarf over my head and ears, clamping my Stetson hat down tight to try and keep my head warm, but it didn't really matter; I was still icy cold.

Quartering back and forth from east to west, I began to find cattle. I pushed and yelled to roust them out, swinging the end of my rope down on their tails to keep them moving. Back and forth I went until I had gathered fifteen head of cows with their calves. It was hard work for horse and rider, for the cattle kept trying to turn aside to hide in the breaks or thickets of cedar. I had to move the sorrel constantly to keep them headed in the right direction.

I knew that Fat Charlie would be doing the same thing east of me, while other cowboys would be combing the breaks to the west, but under the overcast sky and swirling sleet it seemed that the horse and I were all alone. The norther kept on blowing. It helped in one way, for the cattle were not about to turn back into that wind, but the cold was really bad. It sapped the horse's strength, and made me wish I was still on the job in that shoe store in Wichita Falls.

When I was sixteen, I decided I was tired of working on ranches in the long hot summers and cold winters of North Texas. I figured if I got a town job in the summer, I'd be set for indoor work during the winter while going to Rider High School. My cowboy friends laughed at me, but I was determined, and I started looking for work.

Of course I didn't know anything about employment services or resumes, and I'd never done anything for pay that didn't involve cattle or horses, so without any experience I decided I'd just take the first job offered to me. With that plan in mind I went downtown and began to go from store to store asking for a job. After many rejections, I finally hit a winner at the Select Shoe Store on Brazos Street.

The owner was a small, prim man, meticulously dressed. His black hair was slicked back and glistened with hair cream. He affected a pencil line mustache on his mean looking face, and a slightly feminine manner; maybe "fastidious" would be a better word than feminine. Tall for my age, with broad shoulders and a horseman's lean hips, I towered over the owner by several inches. That seemed to intimidate him at first, but then he bristled, rising up on his toes to appear taller. I guess he figured since he was a businessman and I was a poor-looking cowboy, he was better than me, even though I happened to be taller.

I was dressed in my school clothes – Wranglers, a white long-sleeved shirt, boots and hat. My clothes were clean, my mother insisted on that, but not new by a long shot. The shoe store owner kind of tilted his head back and looked down his nose at me, but at least he didn't run me off like everyone else had.

It kind of surprised me, but I was hired after my interview with Mr. Wisel, pronounced with a long "i", and told to appear for work the next morning at 8:00 wearing appropriate clothes.

The next morning I arrived at the store fifteen minutes early. Mrs. Wisel unlocked the door and let me in with a welcoming smile. She was an attractive dark-haired woman in her forties, somewhat taller than her husband, but very quiet and unassuming. I was dressed in my church pants and a white shirt, but I was still wearing boots, for I didn't own any shoes. I thought they looked okay though, because I'd polished them up and pulled my pants legs down over the tops. I held my hat in my hand when I entered the store.

"You can put your hat here, Joe," Mrs. Wisel said, as she showed me the back room, "and then sweep the front walk." I left my hat where she pointed and went back to the front of the store with a broom in my hand. Unlocking the door, I went out to sweep the front walk. When I finished the front, I went back into the store to, at Mrs. Wisel's direction, sweep out the stock room. While I was sweeping, Mr. Wisel came into the room and watched me work. He looked like he had a burr under his saddle, and he wore a displeased look on his face.

"Mr. Garth, you came without references so I don't expect too much from you, but I would have thought you should be able to sweep without explicit instructions."

I stopped and looked down at the owner. "What do you want me to do different, Mr. Weasel?"

"The name is Wisel! And I don't want to hear you mispronounce it again!" and the little man actually stamped his foot. Since I had deliberately mispronounced the name, it was hard to keep my face straight, but I managed.

"Yes, sir," I replied. "What is it about my sweeping that you don't approve of, Mr. *Wisel*?"

Wisel pointed down at the floor at imagined dust. "Look at that! Sweep this room again, and do it right this time!"

That was the first day, and it didn't get any better. I never understood why Wisel hired me, unless it was to be his whipping boy. Didn't really matter much, for I only lasted from Tuesday to Friday, not quite a week. On Friday morning, Mr. Wisel again told me what a sloppy sweeper I was, demanding that I sweep the storeroom for a third time. "Can't you do anything right, boy? You're a totally worthless sweeper, you can't sell shoes, just what can you do?!" the store owner yelled in his high-pitched voice, standing on his tiptoes, shaking a fist in my face, and then pushing me.

While he was shouting at me, Mrs. Wisel looked in and gave me a small, sad smile over her husband's turned shoulder. That did it. I'd seen *The Weasel*, as I secretly called my employer, treating his wife like dirt on several occasions, and town job or not, that Friday I decided that I wasn't going to put up with the little rat any longer.

Since he was demanding to know what I could do right, I decided to show him. I threw the broom at the little man, following it with a hard swung right fist. The owner hit the floor, blood flying from his broken nose, and I hit the street, unemployed, but relatively satisfied, followed by groans from The Weasel, and a huge smile of appreciation from his wife.

I shook my head at the memory, and kept pushing cows in the cold, grinning ruefully at myself. I'd known from the first that I'd never make a shoe salesman, but I reckoned everybody and everything suffered from delusions of grandeur at some time or other. "I suppose you think it'd be better to be a race horse, huh, Red?" I muttered to the sorrel. "You could be in a nice warm barn with nothing to do but run around all day eating your head off. Well, forget it friend. You and me just ain't cut out for the high life." The horse cocked an ear back as if he was listening to me, but he didn't reply.

By the time I'd gathered about thirty head of cattle, I knew I couldn't handle any more, so I stopped searching the draws and breaks, and concentrated on getting my small herd to the pens. Daylight was struggling to replace full darkness when I started out, but it hadn't been very successful. The sky was a mass of dark clouds, the wind increased its howl, and there was no sun. Now instead of being cold night, it was cold day. No real difference to my thinking.

I swung my rope, yipping at the cattle, weaving the sorrel back and forth to keep them bunched and moving to the southwest. My legs were numbed by the cold, and I couldn't feel my feet in the stirrups, though I assumed they were still there since I hadn't fallen out of the saddle. Even with the heavy cotton scarf pulled over my ears under my hat, the long ends wrapped around my neck, my ears were still ice cold, and my face was without feeling.

Up ahead and off to the right I saw a dim light through the sleet. At least I thought it was a light; not just my mind playing tricks on me. It was late-morning by my reckoning. I pushed the cattle forward, and they began to pick up their pace. Now the light was stronger, and I could see the dim shapes of pickups and trailers. I had made it to the Midway Pens.

I tried to call out when I got closer to the pens, but my voice was only a croak. Then, when I had about given up, I saw men on horses come out of the mist of sleet headed my way. The foreman called out, "Go to the shack and get warm, Garth. We'll take care of the cattle." I nodded, or thought I did, lifted the hand that held my rope, and nudged the sorrel off to the side.

There was a shack over there with lights in the windows. I headed for the hitch rail in front of the building and stopped the horse, but when I went to swing my right leg over the cantle, something wasn't working. My right foot seemed to be stuck in the stirrup. Now what? Right then the door of the shack opened and Tom came out bundled up and wrapped like a well-smoked ham.

"Hold on, Joe. Let me get your foot out of the stirrup," he said, easing my right boot out and down. I swung my leg over and slid to the ground, but my feet were so numb I couldn't feel them. I held onto the saddle for just a moment, and then stepped away, stamping until I began to feel the needles of returning circulation. "I'll take care of your horse, Joe. Go on in and have some stew and coffee."

"Thanks, Tom,"

The inside of the rickety shack was as warm and steamy as a sauna compared to the outside. I stepped just to the inside of the door and stood there, pulling off my ice encrusted hat and shaking it out on the floor. Then I unwound my scarf and zipped my jacket open, shrugging it off. I knew that the warm clothes needed to come off or when I went back into the cold, I'd really feel it. My spurs jingled as I stomped my feet, still trying to get the blood to flow.

There were two other cowboys in the building sitting hunched on boxes with their hands wrapped around steaming coffee cups. They nodded to me, but no one spoke. We all knew that this was just a short respite from the day's work. The door slammed open and Fat Charlie came in. "Wow!" he yelled. "Makes a man wonder what he did with his summer wages, don't it?" Charlie was a talker. He wasn't really fat, he just carried a small roll above his belt, but to the rest of us lean riders, that made him *fat*, so we tagged him with the nickname.

One of the other cowboys said, "I know what you did with *your* summer wages, Charlie. I saw you with that little red-headed gal from the Pioneer Lounge. She got all your money, and now she's snug in her bed while you're out here in the cold."

Everybody laughed, and Charlie ruefully shook his head. "She swore she'd be true to me forever, but I guess forever has a price tag on it. Soon as she had my roll, she took off with a long, tall used car salesman!"

We all laughed loudly at that comment. One of the cowboys poured two cups of coffee from the pot on top of the glowing potbellied stove in one corner of the room and brought them to Fat Charlie and me. I'd already taken my heavy gloves off and dropped them on the floor, so I turned to help pull Charlie's off before accepting the cup. "Thanks, Bob," I said. I thought to myself that if I ever got rich I'd sit by the fire on a day like this and *hire* some other fool cowboy to freeze nearly to death gathering cattle in a blue norther. Then I laughed at myself. At $900.00 a month it wasn't likely that would ever happen.

Matt Walters shouldered his way through the door followed by four more frozen cowboys. The little shack was full now, and I began to scoop some of Handy's thick beef stew into bowls for all the cowboys. The foreman brought the stew with him from the home ranch in a large canister, and it smelled great. The taste matched the smell, but we ate fast, knowing that our time here was short, for we had to gather the rest of the cattle and be at the South Pens before dark.

"The hands are switching saddles over in the horse pen right now," Walters said. "You boys got a good gather, and we'll be trailering the cattle from here down to the South Pens. Comb out the breaks good between here and there. When you reach the pens Handy'll have a meal waiting for you. You can leave anytime you want – within the next ten minutes."

I said, "Thanks, Boss. That's real generous of you. You sure we can take the whole ten or do you want change back?"

Walters just grinned at me, and went out, closing the door behind him. Soon, all of us were bundled up again and stepping up on fresh, but very reluctant horses. We left the Midway Pens headed south, spreading out to the east and west as we rode. I looked back in a few minutes, but I couldn't see any lights at the pens through the moisture. Sleet mixed with snow was coming faster now, slashing at us with a meanness that had to be felt to be believed, and the wind was colder than ever.

The cold day wore on and I wondered if it would ever end. I gathered cattle from the breaks, and pushed them on, riding a wide strip back and forth until there were nearly too many to handle, and then I settled down to make sure none of them cut away to one side or the other. Finally, in waning daylight, I saw the dim lights of the South Pens. Once again, Walters came out to meet me with some ranch hands to bring the cattle to the pens, and again Tom helped me out of the saddle, but at least this time I knew that my day was over. Tom took my horse, and I stumbled off to the bunkhouse with relief.

CHAPTER TWO

During the night, the storm blew itself out, and morning dawned bright but cold. The icy chill of the north wind was still bitter, but at least there was no longer snow and sleet filling the air, and a pale sun promised warmth sooner or later, probably way later. The remains of the frozen moisture of the previous day lay now in white humps up against buildings and fence posts. There was no melting, however, since the temperature was still below freezing, and it looked like the ice would be around for a while.

After the cold of yesterday it felt good to be in a warm room standing in a row of half-dressed cowboys, shaving with gear brought down by Handy and his helpers from headquarters. The bunkhouse at the South Pens was not elaborate like the one at Slash T headquarters, but it was sure enough warm. All of the men, cowboys and ranch hands alike, slept in the same large room. On the west side of the bunkroom a door opened into the dining room and kitchen. When I finished shaving, I walked on into the dining room, after putting on my shirt and hat.

The table was already heaped with platters of eggs and sausage, so I loaded my plate and began to eat. Yesterday had been a hungry day and a cold one, and a full stomach meant a warm body. When I was full at last, I sat back and joshed Handy for a bit while he finished his coffee. Too soon Walters came in and began to give assignments for the day.

Matt was a good foreman, fifty if he was a day, and his brown wrinkled face showed the years of outside work in sun and wind. He was bald as an egg on top, and his long arms waved around when he talked, but we liked and respected him, and he could take a wise-guy comment with the best of them.

"Garth and Bryce, you do the roping. White and Rawlins at the branding fires. Williams and Sloan, vaccinations, and stop breaking so many needles! Give those shots while the calves are still down. Rowdy, you cut, earmark and disinfect, and Jake will move the cattle back.

"You ranch hands will help cut the calves away from their mamas, and hold them down at the branding fires. You'll also tend the gates where the cowboys need you. I'll be around to help wherever. Now, we've got a lot of calves to work, and some cows to doctor. We'll do the calves first. The yearlings will be sorted for shipping when we're done with the calves.

"Okay, let's get at it." We all shrugged into our heavy clothes and followed the foreman out.

I was happy to see that the ranch hands brought Buck down to the South Pens when they brought the extra horses the day before. When calf roping was to be done, I wanted to do it from Buck's back whenever possible. While I saddled up, the hands sorted the cattle out of a large pen into a smaller one to get them ready.

There were about four hundred head of cows, calves and yearlings in the pen. These were crowded into an approach funnel that squeezed them into a narrow chute. Gates along this chute were opened or closed as necessary to cut the stock into three groups. When the cows and yearlings were cut away, only the young calves were fed through the end of the chute and out into another large pen.

This was the last of the fall gather. We had been rounding up the cattle for several weeks, but now, finally, we were nearing the end. The Slash T ran over three thousand mother cows, plus bulls and calves. Each year a spring and fall roundup took place to work the cattle and ship the ones that were ready. Cattle sales made up the bulk of the ranch's income.

I mounted and made my way through a gate in the high fence held open by Tom. "Go get 'em, Joe," he called. I grinned at him, touching my hat brim with the fingers of my right hand in salute.

Two propane-fired branding stoves were set up about twenty yards apart, and men stood near them warming themselves, waiting for calves to be dragged up to them. Fat Charlie and I walked our horses into the herd of calves bunched to one side of the large round pen to begin roping them out.

Roping calves at a branding is far different from rodeo tie-down roping. The object is to catch the calves by the hind feet and slowly pull them over to a branding fire. It takes quiet, sure-handed ropers and steady horses to catch the animals one after the other.

At the Slash T, calves were always to be handled as easily as possible to keep injuries down. The owner figured the hands could take care of themselves, but if anyone hurt a cow or calf with rough or careless handling, that man was headed for the highway.

Once a calf was dragged to the fire, the men on the ground would turn the animal so his left side was up for branding and release the cowboy's rope from the calf's heels. Then two men would drop down on the calf, one with a knee on the neck and a foreleg folded and held up, and the other seated on the ground with the top leg hugged to his chest, and his heels pushing the bottom leg away. In this manner, the calf was held securely while a branding iron was laid on his left hip, a needle was pushed into the skin on his neck for a blackleg shot, a sharp knife castrated the bull calves, and an earmark, an under slope, was cut into the left ear.

With a well-oiled team, all of these operations were accomplished in a matter of a few minutes. When the job was done, the calf was released, hazed off to one side of the pen to be pushed into the large corral where the cows were kept. Calf and mother soon matched up, and a lot of bawling and licking of wounds took place.

Charlie and I worked steadily, roping the legs of the calves and dragging them to the fires. By noontime, there were only twenty calves left to work. Handy rang an iron triangle to let us know dinner was ready, and everyone stopped to take care of the horses and make things secure before we ate.

The morning had steadily warmed up as we worked, and by noon the wind was blowing from the south, a softer wind, still holding some cold but with a promise of warmth. When we trooped into the dining room, we began to shed our heavy clothes and sit at the long benches on each side of the table. There was very little talk as cowboys and ranch hands pulled chicken-fried steaks onto their plates off the high-piled platter in the center of the table and dug into the huge bowl of mashed potatoes. Once seated we all poured cream gravy, made in the frying pans for flavor, over steak and potatoes.

There was also a large bowl of creamed corn and an even larger one of peas on the table. These passed up and down with all of us adding to our plates. A tray of hot light-bread biscuits completed the feast. Soon, the only sound in the room was the clash of knives and forks as hungry men cut and scooped, eating the good food.

When our stomachs were mostly filled up, Matt Walters, seated at the end of the table, spoke up. "We've only got a few calves to finish after dinner, so you boys at the south fire can put your stuff up and start doctoring the cows. Joe, you do the last of the roping, and Charlie, you help cut out the cows that are hurt. Once all the cow work is done, the ranch hands will feed the cattle in the shipping pens, and the cowboys can go back to headquarters with Handy. When the ranch hands come in they'll bring the horses. This is Friday, and the shipping trucks won't be here until Monday, so tomorrow will be a day off.

"Now, just because I'm giving you an extra half day off doesn't mean you can go honky tonkin' all weekend. Monday morning we'll be back down here early to help load the trucks. We've got two hundred head of feeders and yearlings to load so we'll need every man to help. I want all of you back on the ranch by Sunday midnight, and nobody better be sick on Monday morning!"

We listened to the foreman's speech with barely suppressed good humor. The weather was breaking, and we were looking at two whole days ahead to take in the delights of Wichita Falls, Texas, such as they were. In fact, if we finished up early enough today some of the cowboys might just go on in to town and get a head start.

The work went fast in the afternoon, and it was well before dark when we made it back to headquarters. Several of the men got slicked up and headed right off for town, but I decided to wait until Saturday morning. After the last two hard days I wanted a good night's sleep in my own warm bunk to recover. I wondered if that was a sign that I was getting old. No, couldn't be. I was only in my mid-thirties after all. That wasn't old, was it?

When I came into the dining room at eight the next morning for a late breakfast, I was dressed in my town clothes, new shirt and Wranglers, gleaming black full-quill ostrich-hide boots, and a black belt with small conchos set around it.

"Hey, Handy!" I called out. "How about some eggs?"

The cook came out of the kitchen also dressed in town clothes to announce, "I'm done cookin' for the weekend, Joe. If you want eggs, you'll have to ask Jose." Handy poured two cups of coffee and brought them to the table, sitting down across from me.

I grinned at him. "Why, Handy Otler, you look almost human." I wrinkled my nose and sniffed. "You even *smell* almost human."

"That's no compliment coming from *you*," he replied. "You've been around horses and cows so much, you don't even *know* what a human being smells like."

I lifted my voice and called out, "Hey, Joe! How about some eggs?"

A young man put his head around the doorframe and smiled all over his face. "You bet, Jose!" It was a joke between us. My name in Spanish was the same as the cook's, and we often played the name game. "How many you want?"

"Better have four or five, and maybe some sausage. I may not get around to eatin' dinner today."

The assistant cook's head disappeared, and we heard him begin to sing *Spanish Eyes* while cracking eggs into a skillet.

"How about a ride into town, Joe?" Handy asked.

"Sure. I'll be goin' in once Jose fills me up." My Ford pickup was ten years out of the show room and somewhat dented, but it still ran. Except for my clothes, the truck, my horse and gear, and a rusty stock trailer made up my entire estate.

We'd all been paid on Friday, and since few of us owned bank accounts, the ranch's accountant cashed our checks for us. After taxes, I had a bit over $800.00 in my pocket, and Handy would have more, since cooks were considered skilled labor and paid higher than cowboys.

Handy sat with me until I finished my breakfast, and then followed me out the door. In a few minutes we were bowling along FM 1440. When that road connected to U.S. Highway 62/83, we'd only be sixteen miles from Childress, Texas. Of course, Childress was not our goal. That was the town where the Slash T and other ranches in the area bought their supplies, but it didn't offer much in the way of entertainment, at least cowboy entertainment. Once we reached Childress we would hit the main road, U.S. Highway 287, for Wichita Falls, Texas, the nearest big town in the area.

I kept my foot down, and the old pickup ate up the miles to Childress. Once on 287, a good four-lane freeway, I really opened the truck up and we tore down the road toward the city. "Joe, don't you think 90 is a little fast?" Handy asked, a bit of a quaver in his voice. "I want to get to town, too, but I'd like to get there in one piece." He asked his question when we were passing an eighteen-wheeler like it was sitting still.

I laughed and replied, "Just open the door and get out anytime you think I'm goin' too fast, Handy. I won't take any offense." The speedometer needle stayed where it was. Handy grumbled a bit, but he didn't make any more remarks about speed.

Usually the highway between Vernon and Wichita Falls was well covered by the state police, but not today. I was slowing down for Iowa Park before we saw the first DPS car, and since I was down to seventy-five miles an hour the state trooper didn't pay any attention to us.

The Saturday morning streets of Wichita Falls were nearly deserted. I pulled into the parking lot of a convenience store, stopping at the gas pumps. Handy got out to go in, and I followed when the tank was full. I paid the cashier for the gas, and the young man said, "Want to buy a lottery ticket? The big one is up to ten million."

"Ten million what?" I asked.

"Dollars," the clerk replied.

"How much does a ticket cost?"

"Depends on what you want." He went on to explain the lottery system, but I didn't really pay much attention. The clerk ended with, "Or you could play Mega Millions, which starts at twelve million and just goes on up. How about it?"

I said, "Well, let's keep the money in Texas; give me what I need for the Texas Lotto."

The clerk pulled off the ticket and showed me where to check QP to let the terminal pick the numbers for me. I also chose the *Cash Option.* "If I win, I want it all," I told the clerk, as if I handled that kind of money all the time. When I got out to the pickup I tossed the ticket into the glove compartment. Handy said, "Did he sucker you into buying a lotto ticket?"

"Sure did. Who knows, I might just win millions of bucks and quit cowboying."

"Uh-huh. And pigs might just sprout wings and fly, too."

The weekend went by quickly. Handy and I returned to the ranch about 10:00 Sunday night. We hadn't done anything wild in the city, but we'd still managed to spend plenty of money.

The weather had changed completely by the time the cattle trucks began backing into the loading chutes at the South Pens on Monday morning. The sun was shining with some real warmth, and the cowboys and ranch hands were working in their shirtsleeves. The old timers' saying was sure right: "*If you don't like the weather in Texas, just wait a bit, and it'll change.*"

The loading went well. Fat Charlie and I were mounted on quiet horses along with two other cowboys, and we slowly worked the feeders toward the narrow end of the pen they were in. Down at that end there were two more cowboys on horseback crowding the cattle into an approach to the loading chute. Standing on the fence were several ranch hands with long poles. They prodded the cattle up the loading chute and into the trucks. The word "cowpuncher" was coined in the 1800's by trainmen who watched cowboys with long poles "punching" cattle into the railcars.

The morning work went on and the sun gained in strength. Dust began to boil up in the pen, and I pulled a large handkerchief out of my pocket and tied it over the lower half of my face. Truck after truck was loaded and pulled away.

We all stopped work at noon and ate a meal prepared by Handy and Jose; Handy fixed his good chicken-fried steaks with lots of mashed potatoes and gravy, and Jose topped the meal off with a baked apple cobbler.

Back at work after dinner, the last truck was filled, and we began to load the horses into trailers for the ride back to headquarters.

Tuesday morning Fat Charlie and I were sent to the West Pasture to check on waterholes and fences, along with Tom Hansen and another ranch hand named Nubbin. Tom drove the pickup pulling a trailer with two horses in it, but Nubbin was just along for the ride.

When we crossed the bridge over the Middle Pease River south of CeeVee, I said, "Tom, do you ever run the road grader that maintains the ranch roads?"

"No, but Nubbin does, don't you Nub?"

Nubbin was not a talker; he just grunted, his way of communicating most of the time. It was up to the listener to decide whether the grunt meant yes or no.

"Why do you want to know who drives the road grader, Joe?" Tom asked.

"Because these ranch roads are all so rough. Whoever does the work does a lousy job. Why, a couple of weeks ago Charlie and I picked up a cow that'd just dropped a calf out at Severs Tank, and before we got her back to the ranch the road shook her so bad the calf was sucking pure butter out of her bag." Tom laughed at my exaggeration, and Nubbin actually smiled a little bit.

When we reached the end of the road, Tom and Nubbin helped us unload the horses, and then unhitched the trailer.

They would drive down the fence line looking for breaks while Fat Charlie and I rode out to check on water holes.

The weather was warm enough with just a slight wind from the south, but in this country that could change in a heart beat, so while we both rode in shirtsleeves, there were heavy coats tied behind our saddles.

Noontime came and went as we rode from one dirt tank to another. These tanks were nothing more than round hollows scraped out of the ground near some dry creek or wash. When the rains came, the water would run down the gullies and into the tank, making a water catch that would last for some time, depending on how hot the weather was and how many cattle were drinking from the supply, and, of course, how long it was between rains.

The term "blue" attached to the word "norther" means some form of moisture driven by a cold wind out of the north. However, the blue norther that made our lives so miserable during the last day of the gather brought sleet and light snow with it, but no rain. There is very little moisture in sleet, and not much more in snow, and there'd been little rain in the weeks before the norther hit. Most of the tanks and waterholes we checked were either dry or nearly so.

We ran across a few cows and steers in the area, but not many. We knew that the foreman was wondering if this part of the ranch would hold more cattle, but I doubted if it would stand more than were already feeding on it.

By mid-afternoon we'd made a large circle in the pasture, and we rode on back to the road where the trailer waited. The ranch hands hadn't returned, so we loosened cinches and sat on the south side of the trailer enjoying the sunshine. "Joe, what would you do if you came into a lot of money?" Fat Charlie asked.

"Well, I sure wouldn't be out here in the middle of nowhere checkin' on water holes," I replied.

"Okay, so what would you do?"

I thought for a bit. "I'd buy a ranch and raise the best Black

Angus cattle and Quarter Horses in the country. Then I'd sure enough hire somebody to do all the work. Every day I'd ride around and just enjoy watching my horses and cows, and maybe go to a few rodeos or something; but I'd never again hear old Matt's voice wakin' me up before daybreak. How about you?"

Charlie laughed, and said, "I wouldn't have a ranch at all. Seems to me that even if you're the owner you have to worry about a whole lot of things like prices and weather and payin' wages. No sir. Not me. I'd buy a motel and let people come and pay me for staying in my rooms I'd just sit behind the desk and rake in the money, and anything that needed doing I'd hire done. Yep, that's what I'd do. And if I decided I didn't cotton to the motel business, I'd just sell out and loaf around all day."

"Now the problem for you, Charlie, is that if you didn't have any work to do, you'd *really* get fat. And you know women don't like big fat men. Why look at how that red head that you were running around town with last summer traded you in for a skinny car salesman, and you're just a little bit fat!"

Charlie pulled off his hat and whopped me in the chest with it, and we were wrestling around on the ground like a couple of kids when the ranch hands drove up laughing at us. We stopped fooling around, grinned at each other, brushed the dirt off our clothes and loaded the horses.

The next day Charlie and I were back in the same section checking more water holes. When we came in late that afternoon, I told Matt that there was not enough water to send any more cows to that part of the range. "We can look further south tomorrow if you want Matt, but things are really dry out there. I don't think that section got much moisture from the last rain we got a month ago, or any before that."

"Thanks, Joe. I reckon you're right. Tomorrow, you and Charlie can go down south of the river and check on water holes there."

That evening all of us cowboys were gathered around the TV in our living room watching the news on Channel 3. Just before an ad, the announcer said, "We'll give you the winning lottery numbers after these messages."

Handy wandered in and leaned on the doorframe. "Hey, Joe!" he called. "Where's that lottery ticket you bought the other day?"

I turned and looked at him. "Still out in the pickup, I guess."

"Well, why don't you go get it and see if you won the lottery?"

With my boots off I was laid back in one of the recliners just as comfortable as all get out. "Too much trouble," I replied. "Besides, nobody ever really wins the lottery. The state just makes up phony names and announces they're winners, and then they keep all the money. You know that lottery is crooked."

The ads ended and the TV announcer came back on. "The Texas Lottery is worth ten million dollars today, and here are the winning numbers: *3 22 8 17 9*." Those numbers came up on the screen superimposed over little white balls.

Handy took a pencil from behind his ear and wrote the numbers down in a tally book. "Give me your keys," he said. "I'll go check on your ticket."

I dug out my keys and tossed them to him. Handy was gone for a few minutes, and then we all heard him whoop. He ran back through the door and yelled, "Joe! You're the winner! The numbers all match on your ticket! You just won the Texas Lottery!"

CHAPTER THREE

When I heard Handy's shout, I stood right up and looked at him with my mouth hanging open. At first, the idea of winning the lottery just didn't register, but then the other men began to shout out their congratulations and slap me on the back, and I realized that something fantastic had just happened. My first words were, "What do I do now?"

"You go back to the store where you bought your ticket and show it to somebody," Handy said.

"You mean that store owner is goin' to give me ten million dollars?"

"Of course not. Nobody has that much money lying around. The store man will okay your ticket, and you take it to Austin and cash it in," Handy replied.

I digested his words slowly. I looked at the clock above the TV and saw that it was 10:30. "I guess I better wait until morning to go in. That convenience store's probably closed now."

The others urged me to go that night and get my ticket validated, but I still wasn't too sure anything would come of it, so I tucked the ticket into my wallet and went to bed.

The next morning I was up early with excitement building in my soul. What if there really was something to this lottery business, and I'd actually won something? I didn't really believe in the ten million dollars, but even a thousand wouldn't hurt.

I shaved carefully, dressed in my town clothes and went up to the foreman's house and knocked on the front door. Walters' wife answered the door, and I asked to see the boss. When Matt heard it was me, he called out, "Come on in, Joe."

In the kitchen I said good morning to Mrs. Walters and accepted a cup of coffee. "What's on your mind this early, Garth?" Walters asked.

I took out the lottery ticket and showed it to the foreman. "I'm not too sure there's anything to this lottery business, Matt, but if there is, I'd sure hate to miss out on ten million dollars. With that much I'd be able to buy a new shirt or two."

Matt laughed long and loud. "Actually, Joe, you can buy the factory that makes the shirts and the store that sells them." He thought for a minute, and then said, "Normally, I'd only let a cowboy go to town on a workday if he had a problem of some kind that couldn't wait for the weekend, but I guess we can call this a personal crisis, so go on into town and check on your ticket. Be back here tonight, though, or let me know if you're not comin' back. If you're headed for Austin I'd like to know about it."

I went back to the bunkhouse and slowly packed a few things in a sports bag in case I was gone overnight. The cowboys were up, and of course they all shot a wise crack or two my way, but I ignored them and finally made it out to my pickup. I didn't rush into Wichita Falls though, obeying the speed limit all the way, and pulling into the convenience store just before 11:00 a.m. There were several people in the store, so I waited until my turn came at the counter. Then I showed my ticket to the clerk and said in a quiet voice that I thought I'd won the lottery. The clerk quickly checked the winning numbers and shouted even louder than Handy. "We have a winner!" he yelled out, and every head in the store turned to stare at me.

Hearing the noise, the manager came out of a back room and took the ticket from the clerk, checking the numbers to be sure there was no mistake. Then he reached across the counter and shook my hand up and down. "Jake's right, mister. You are the winner!"

The manager took a photocopy of the ticket, validated it, and wrote down my name and address. Then he said, "All claims for the big one have to go to Austin. Take your ticket, guard it carefully, and go on down to Austin and cash it in. Here's where you go." He handed me a detailed map of the state capital.

Still amazed that the whole thing was real, I put the ticket back in my wallet and left the store. In the parking lot, I climbed into the pickup and sat for a few minutes thinking about what to do next. If I went back to the ranch, I'd just have to turn around and come back this way to go to Austin, so I decided to call the foreman instead. Getting back out of the truck, I went to the pay phone on the corner of the building and called the Slash T.

Matt wasn't at home or in his office, but I left word for him that I was going down to Austin and didn't know for sure when I'd be back, but I'd let him know when I was in range. I also said to tell Walters that I'd understand if he felt the need to dock my pay. Since the story of my winning ticket had quickly gone the rounds of the ranch, the secretary at Matt's office laughed at the mention of pay, and she was till laughing when I put the phone down and went back to the truck. It was a long ways to Austin, but I figured I'd make a start right now.

I motored right along, stopping early for the night at a motel on the south side of Waco. The next morning I was up early, had my breakfast and headed on down Interstate 35. I'd never been to the state capital before, and even following the map the store manager gave me, it was late morning when I finally arrived at the Texas Lottery Commission Headquarters on East 6th Street, after taking several wrong turns. I left my pickup in a parking lot nearby, and entered the building. The receptionist pointed me to the right office, and I went in to present my ticket.

The first person I talked to checked the numbers on my ticket and started the ball rolling, and I was never just too sure of the sequence of events that followed. I was ushered into a large room with windows all along one wall, and offered a soft chair and a cup of coffee. While I sipped the coffee, people came and went, some asking me questions, and some giving me advice. Mostly, I didn't know what they were talking about, so I just smiled a lot and nodded.

Evidently someone had called the newspapers and TV stations, for before long the room was filled up with reporters and camera crews. Camera flashes went off, and I was told to stand here, or sit there. Finally, after what seemed hours, all of the media people were ushered out of the room, and I was alone with a thin young man in a black suit holding a cashier's check out to me.

"This is a check made out to you, Mr. Garth. The amount is $4,110,396.42. You can take this to any bank and deposit it."

I looked at the check. The numbers didn't really mean

anything to me at first, but then they did and I said, "I thought I won ten million. What happened to the rest of it?"

The young man looked pained. Who was this down at heels cowboy to question the great authority of the Texas Lottery Commission? "Yes, Mr. Garth, the base amount was ten million dollars. However, since you chose the Cash Option, we deduct the amount that would have been available to you over a twenty-five year payout, plus income tax. The net amount comes to $4,110,396.42."

I looked the young man right in the eyes. "Sonny," I said, "where I come from we don't have a lot of money, and we don't know much about big bucks, but what we promise we deliver. I've got a feelin' that somebody just cheated me out of half my winnings, but I guess when you're talking all these zeros, it don't matter much. I'll just take what's left here and go on about my business."

The clerk didn't answer, he just watched with a strange look on his face as I made my way out of the room.

I left the building thinking to myself, "I knew this lottery deal was crooked, I just didn't know *how* crooked. Oh well, I've been rolled before, and I reckon this won't be the last time."

It was not until I was headed north up I-35 and almost to Temple that it really began to sink in: *I am the newest millionaire in Texas!* Great, but what in the world was I going to do with over four million dollars?

CHAPTER FOUR

It was late Saturday evening when I arrived back at the ranch. I went first to the foreman's home to let Walters know I was back. "Well, Joe, did they give you the money?"

I grinned. "Yep, at least as much as was left after they took their share."

Matt motioned to a chair and sat down on the couch facing me. "Well, what are you goin' to do now? I reckon you've come to give me notice."

"Matt, I don't know what I'm going to do for sure, but Monday I've got to deposit the check in a bank. Then I reckon I'll have to see what offers. I've never had more than wages in my life before, so I guess I'll have to talk to some financial folks for advice. Maybe a banker can help me out."

The foreman looked long at me, and then said, "Joe, you're a top hand with horses and cattle, and you are steadier than some of the cowboys on the Slash T, not nearly as quick to throw your money away on liquor and women. Now, I don't like to lose a good cowboy, but I know you can't sit on several million dollars and still be a cowboy at this ranch, so I'll help out any way I can.

"You've been a good hand, and I know Mr. Tomlinson would wish you the best. We're not short handed now with the fall gather being finished, so you're quitting won't hurt us much. When do you want to draw your pay?"

"Well, I reckon I'll take it now, if you don't mind, Matt," I replied. "After I do my banking, I'd kind of like to look around for a place of my own. Could I leave Buck here until I have a place for him? I'd be glad to pay for his board."

"Just leave him where he is and come get him when you want, Joe. And there won't be a bill. I reckon he's earned his keep for a while."

We went over to Matt's office and I collected what little pay I had coming, and then I went to the bunkhouse to get my gear. Since it was Saturday, most of the cowboys were gone, but Handy was there kicked back in a recliner. "Hey, Joe. Come back to see how us poor folks live?"

I grinned at my old friend. "From now on, Mr. Otler, call my secretary and ask for an appointment if you want to talk to me."

Handy threw a magazine at me. "Why would I want to talk to you, you worthless cow nurse?"

I went on into the bunkroom and began to put my stuff together, and Handy followed, leaning on the doorframe and watching me pack. "You going to take your saddle, too, Joe?"

Good question. I stopped rolling socks and sat down on the bed. "Not today, Handy. Matt says I can leave Buck here until I have place for him, and I reckon I'll leave my gear, too. Monday I want to begin looking for a place to buy, and when I'm set, I'll come back and get my things.

"Goin' to miss seeing your ugly face everyday, though. When I get settled, how about comin' for a visit?"

"Wouldn't miss it for the world. What kind of place you lookin' for?"

"Well, I've always thought that if a rich uncle died that I didn't know about and left me a bunch of money, I'd like to have a horse ranch. You know, a good stud and some mares, maybe breed other folks mares for them. Maybe a few head of Black Angus for beef. I don't know where I'm going to find such a place, but I wouldn't mind it bein' around Wichita Falls or Graham, maybe. I never had a rich uncle, but maybe the State of Texas will do just as well."

Handy picked up one of my bags and headed out the door. I dropped my spurs into the other bag, zipped it up and followed him.

At the pickup, we silently shook hands, and Handy turned to walk back to the bunkhouse. As I watched him go, Jose came out of the back door and held up his hand in a salute. "Vaya con Dios, Jose," he called.

"Gracias, amigo," I replied, and I climbed into the pickup and drove out of the ranch yard.

That night I stayed in a motel just outside Wichita Falls. After my trip to Austin I was low on cash, but I figured I'd have enough to clear my bill on Monday morning, and once I went to a bank I'd have plenty of folding money to put in my pockets.

Sunday slipped by, and I napped and snacked my way

through the day, watching football on TV. On Monday morning I loafed around until 9:00, and then went to pay my bill. I wasn't real sure what time banks opened, but I didn't think it would be much before 10:00, so I stopped at a greasy spoon and had a leisurely breakfast.

Sitting at a booth in plain sight, I noticed some of the customers looking at me and nudging each other. Now, what was that all about? Then I bought a newspaper, and as soon as I saw the front page, I knew why they were staring. My face was staring out at me, and the words underneath caught my attention: ***"COWBOY WINS THE BIG ONE!"***

I was suddenly very uncomfortable. I hadn't given a thought to the photographers at the lottery commission headquarters, but evidently they sent pictures all over the state. Now, I always liked my privacy, and I was the last person in the world to seek any kind of fame, unless it was in a rodeo arena. I didn't like crowds much, and I sure didn't like being stared at. Quickly, I finished my breakfast, dropped some money on the table, and went out to the pickup.

It was time to go to the bank, but which bank? I'd had never had a bank account, and I had no idea how to set one up. Sitting in the pickup, I noticed that I was on Kemp Street headed south. Wasn't there a bank on Kemp south of Sikes Center? I started the truck and drove on down the street, and when I came to the intersection with Midwestern Parkway, I could see Sikes Center, a large enclosed mall, on my left, and just south of the mall the sign for the First American Commerce Bank.

The building was a huge block of brick with reflective glass windows, and it looked substantial and solid as I pulled into the parking lot. The front door opened automatically, and closed behind me when I crossed the entryway. Inside there were desks scattered around, with the tellers' cages behind them. I went up to the first desk, and the pretty young woman seated there asked, "May I help you, sir?"

I pulled my hat off and replied, "Well, ma'am, I'd like to open an account."

The young woman pushed a button on her phone and spoke into the microphone near her mouth, and then she motioned me to a chair and said, "Please have a seat, sir. There will be someone here from new accounts right away." I sat down.

The pretty girl went on with her duties, answering the phone and working on some papers on her desk. In a very few minutes, another young woman came to stand in front of me and said, "Did you want to open an account, sir?"

I stood and followed the girl to another desk set in an alcove, thinking, *this bank has a very good judge of women somewhere. This girl's is as pretty as the first one.*

The young woman took her seat behind the desk, pulled a form toward her, and motioned for me to sit down. "Name, please?" she asked.

"Joe Garth."

"Address?"

"Well, I just quit the Slash T Ranch south of Childress, but I don't have a new address yet. I'll be looking for a place to buy."

"I see. Well, let's put down your last address; did you say the Splash Tee?"

"No ma'am. It's a ranch, and the brand is a slash followed by a capital 'T'. The address is Childress, Texas. I don't remember the zip code."

The young woman was busily typing information into her computer. "Phone number?"

"Well, I guess you want the number of the ranch. It's 940-886-9875."

"What kind of account do you want to open, Mr. Garth, checking or savings?"

"How about one of those accounts I've heard of where you get some interest like a savings account, but you can write checks on it like a checking account?"

The girl stopped pecking at the keyboard and looked at me. "We have several different accounts like that, Mr. Garth, but most of them require a rather large amount to open. How much did you want to deposit to start your account?" Up to this point the young woman had been very professional, but now she looked at me with a small smile on her face. She could see I wasn't dressed like a man who'd have much money, and I sure didn't know anything about bank accounts. The young lady looked like she kind of felt sorry for me, and while she didn't want to hurt my feelings, she knew she had to be honest with me.

"Well, ma'am, I reckon I'll want to deposit most of this check, except for a little cash for walking around money," I said as I laid the check from the lottery commission out in front of her.

The pretty young woman gaped at the numbers on the check. Her mouth dropped open, and she quickly looked up at me. "You're the cowboy who won the Texas Lottery, aren't you?" she asked in amazement.

"Yes, ma'am, I reckon I am."

"Please wait right here, Mr. Garth," she said. "I'll have to talk to my manager," and she jumped to her feet and disappeared through a door behind her.

In seconds a large man dressed in an expensive suit came through the door holding my check, with the young woman trailing him. "Mr. Garth!" he boomed. "I'm George Wilkins. Welcome to First American Commercial!"

I stood, and the man grabbed my hand and began to shake it vigorously. "Please come with me," he said as he led the way to the elevator.

"Where are we off to?" I asked.

The elevator doors slid open, and the big man motioned me in. "Why, were going to the bank president's office. Mr. Argus will want to meet you," Wilkins replied. He didn't ask if I wanted to meet the bank president or not, but then it might not be a bad idea. After all, if this bank was going to hold my money, I should meet the man in charge.

When the elevator doors slid open we entered a large lobby with another pretty girl behind a desk. She smiled at Mr. Wilkins as he walked by her and entered a door marked, "Winslow Argus, President."

The room we entered was spacious and well decorated, and a secretary sat behind a desk there. "Julie, please tell Mr. Argus that I'm here with Joe Garth, the man who won the lottery last week."

Julie called, and as she put the phone down, a richly carved door behind her opened and a small man in a pinstripe suit emerged holding his hand out. "Mr. Garth," he said, "welcome to First American Commercial Bank. Please come on back," and he turned to lead the way into his office followed by Wilkins and me. Argus had a mustache, and being small and well groomed, he reminded me of Mr. Wisel, the owner of the shoe store where I'd tried to work as a teenager. I decided I'd hold judgment though until I got to know the man better.

I sat down where Argus directed in an alcove with comfortable chairs around a glass-topped coffee table. Wilkins handed the check to Mr. Argus, and then took a seat himself.

"Well, Mr. Garth," Argus said with a smile plastered on his thin face. "Do you know what you want to do with this money?"

"Like I told the young lady, Mr. Argus, I'd like an account that bears interest but that I can write checks on. Do you have something like that? And I'd like a few hundred dollars for folding money, let's say five hundred to be sure I have enough."

"Certainly we have accounts like that, and the cash is no problem. We have a money market account that bears 4% interest, and you can write as many checks as you want. Shall we go ahead and open that account for you now?"

"Yes," I said. "Do I need to go back downstairs?"

Argus gave me an unctuous smile, and Wilkins laughed aloud. "No, Mr. Garth. We can take care of everything from here." He handed the check to me and asked, "Would you please endorse the check? Wilkins here will open the account and bring the papers for you to sign."

I scrawled my name on the back of the check and handed it to Mr. Wilkins. The new accounts manager left the president's office, and Mr. Argus said, "How about some coffee while we wait, Mr. Garth? And maybe a donut?"

"Coffee will be fine, Mr. Argus," I replied.

In a very short time I was passing through the desks on the ground floor once again, only this time I was escorted by Mr. Argus and Mr. Wilkins. In my pocket I had five crisp one hundred dollar bills, and in my hand I held a temporary checkbook. Wilkins had told me that I would have preprinted checks by Wednesday. If I would just stop by the bank I could pick them up, or, if I preferred, the bank would messenger the checks to me wherever I was. Seemed like they just couldn't do enough for me – or at least for my money.

It was something of a relief to sit in the seat of my familiar old pickup again. The events in the bank seemed very unreal. Was this what it was like to be a celebrity? If it was, I wasn't too sure I liked the position very much.

Across the street from the bank there was a Western Wear store that I had traded at several times, and I thought I might just stop over there and buy a new hat or something. I left the bank parking lot, found a break in the traffic, and pulled up in front of the store. Inside I drew in the pleasant smells of tanned leather and new Wranglers.

A young girl who couldn't have been more than eighteen, dressed in the Hollywood version of cowgirl clothes, Mexican off-the-shoulder blouse, short denim skirt and cowgirl boots, came up to me. "My name is Lori; may I help you?" she asked in a breathy voice.

I grinned at her. "I'll bet you can, Lori," I replied. "Let's start with hats."

Before long I had bought a new Stetson hat, two pairs of Wranglers, three shirts, a wide belt, and two pairs of boots. These items cost more than the $500.00 I had in my pocket, so I pulled out the checkbook and, with Lori's help, wrote my first check.

In the course of shopping, Lori had figured out just who I was, and her manner changed from helpful to hunt-ful. The Mexican blouse had fallen further off the right shoulder, and when she gave me my receipt, she also handed me a piece of paper with her name, address and phone number on it. "Now, you just call me anytime, Joe. I'd really like to see a lot more of you," she gushed.

As the newest millionaire in Wichita Falls, I smiled at her, but I didn't commit myself. She followed me through the door, and as I pulled out of the parking lot, Lori was standing on the front step waving.

CHAPTER FIVE

I decided that I needed a place to stay until I could find a permanent home, so I drove east on Southwest Parkway until I came to the Grace Freeway interchange, and headed north. There was a Hilton Hotel at the north end of town, and I thought

I would go there and get a room.

When I went through the doors of the Hilton I almost turned around and went back out. The lobby was huge and rich, far more so than any motel I'd had ever stayed in, but I decided I might as well learn to indulge in this kind of luxury, and walked on in.

Thanks to the newspapers and TV, the clerk recognized me immediately, and the red carpet was rolled out. Soon I was looking out the window of a seventh-floor suite. My clothes had been hung up by a porter, and, since it was nearly time for dinner – lunch in town talk – I was encouraged to order from the menu. While I waited for my food, I relaxed in a very comfortable recliner. Looking around at the rich furnishings, I thought I might just get used to this easy life if I tried real hard.

Lunch came, and the New York strip steak I had ordered was okay, though not as well done as I cared for. Working around cattle most of my life I'd had seen a lot of bovine blood, but I didn't much like it on my plate.

After I finished eating, I called down and asked the hotel courtesy desk to locate a realtor in the area who handled horse ranches. If this was a strange request for the Hilton representative, he gave no hint, and I was leafing through a magazine when the phone rang. "I have contacted Miles Moore Real Estate for you, Mr. Garth. They claim to specialize in large horse and cattle ranches. Do you want the number or shall I go ahead and call the office and let you know when Mr. Moore is ready to take your call?"

This was new. I didn't even have to dial the phone myself. "Please go ahead and find Mr. Moore, and let me know when he's on the line," I replied.

"Yes, sir."

The phone rang again in thirty minutes, and Miles Moore was quite happy to talk to me about ranches for sale.

Moore entered my suite with a briefcase in one hand, and the other outstretched. "Nice to meet you, Mr. Garth."

I shook the hand and looked the man over. He was dressed in much the same kind of clothes I had on, and the tan line on his forehead showed that he wore a hat outside.

"Same here, Mr. Moore, but I'm not real used to folks calling me 'Mr. Garth.' Please call me Joe."

"Fine, Joe, and I'd appreciate it if you'd call me Miles."

We sat down at the large table in the dining room and I ordered coffee. We chatted about ranches and range conditions until the coffee came, and then we got down to business.

Moore spread out some maps and listing sheets and pointed to an area about ten miles southeast of Wichita Falls just off of U.S. Highway 287. "There's a place here that might interest you. It's a horse breeding and training operation with some cattle on the side. The property's not large, only 1,200 acres, but it's well watered with two year-around creeks and several good tanks. The mesquite's been cleared off, and there are a couple of hay meadows planted to Coastal Bermuda. Most of the pasture has been improved, too.

"The house is fairly large – four thousand square feet – and, while it's about twenty years old, it has recently been totally remodeled. There's a twenty-stall horse barn, and a large hay and cow barn, as well as a covered arena." He slid some photos onto the table and continued, "Here are some pictures of the place."

"How much do they want?" I asked as if I bought property every day of the week.

"One million two, but I think they'll take less. I've spoken recently to the wife, and she wants to sell as soon as possible. I reckon the husband's just as anxious."

One million, two hundred thousand dollars. I almost had to pinch myself to realize that I was actually talking about that kind of money. Just a few days ago I was a nine-hundred dollar a month cowboy, and now I was talking about buying a ranch for over $1,000,000.00. It took some getting used to.

After some discussion, I wanted to see the property, and Miles suggested we go in his pickup. "How come this place is for sale, Miles?" I asked as we drove down the freeway.

"Well, unfortunately it's a divorce case. The folks who own it are breaking up, and neither of them wants the other one to have the ranch, so they're selling, figuring to split up the money, I suppose."

I didn't say anything, but I thought to myself that marriage was an iffy proposition at best. Way too many couples seemed to divorce, and I wondered if they were ever any better off. These thoughts didn't last long, though, because marriage was not something I was very much interested in, and I certainly had no plans of entering that state of unlikely bliss myself.

Miles drove to the little village of Jolly on U.S. 287, and turned south on Farm to Market Road 2393. About four miles down this blacktopped road he pulled into a paved entryway, passed through an imposing power operated stone-pillar gate after entering a code on the keypad, over a cattle guard and stopped the pickup. From this point all of the ranch buildings were in view, and they were situated in a real pretty setting, with rolling hills all around, and large live oak trees shading the house and barns.

We sat there for several minutes, and Miles didn't say anything; he just let me have a long look, and then he started up and drove down the winding drive. The ranch road went on past a short driveway to the house, but Miles turned in and stopped the pickup on the circle drive in front of the imposing home. We both got out and walked up on the long front porch, and Miles pushed the doorbell. Somewhere in the house we could hear a bell toll, and then the opening bars of an instrumental version of *"The Red River Valley."* I ruefully shook my head and vowed that if I bought this place that would be the first thing changed. The song was okay, but hearing those first notes every time someone pushed the doorbell would be way too much.

No one came to answer the door, so Miles took out a key and fitted it into the lock. We entered a wide hallway that led into a living room filled with light. When we passed into the living room, I could see that there were skylights in the vaulted ceiling and the light was natural. Miles said, "Nobody's living here now, but I always like to make sure before I burst into a house. This is the living room, and the dining room and kitchen are through those doors on the east. On the right the open doors lead into the den." We walked that way and I was astounded.

The den was large with light birch picture frame paneling on two walls, and muted paper on another on both sides of a stone fireplace, while the entire east wall was glass from floor to ceiling, with a sliding glass door in the middle leading out onto a large wooden deck. Through the windows I could see the arena, the horse barn, and a great deal of pipe-fenced pasture.

The house was furnished, and I asked, "Does the furniture go with the place?"

"Yes it does," Moore replied. "The sellers have already taken out what they want, so the rest is to go with the house. There are no horses or cattle on the place, as those were sold at auction last week. There is a hired man still here taking care of the ranch until it's sold. He's a cowboy and a horseman, so you might want to keep him on."

Miles went on to show me the office and bedrooms, and then we went out on the deck that curved around the house from east to south, and followed a blacktop path down to the horse barn.

As we entered the long alleyway between the stalls, a cowboy came out of the tack room to meet us. He was probably in his forties, but his weather beaten face made him look older. He was over six feet tall, there was a bit of a stoop to his shoulders, and his legs were kind of bowed. His blue eyes held a twinkle, and his broad smile brightened up the day. He stuck out his hand in true Texas fashion and said, "Howdy. Name's Roy Alcorn."

I shook his hand, and so did Miles. "I'm Miles Moore, and this is Joe Garth," Miles said as he introduced us.

Alcorn grinned wider. "I reckon I know who Joe Garth is. Your picture's been all over the paper and TV lately. You goin' to buy this place?"

"Well, I don't know yet, but I'm thinkin' about it," I replied.

"If you do, I'd like to stay on, that is if you're hirin'. Wouldn't mind workin' for a real cowboy for a change. I heard you worked for the Slash T, that right?"

I nodded. "Sure did, and it's a pretty good outfit, though how they'll get along without me I'll never know." That made Alcorn laugh, and Miles joined him.

With Roy as a guide we looked over the buildings and pens. The place was set up very well, with the arena and barn for horses, and large working and feeding pens for cattle. "Can't really show you the pastures since they sold off the horses, but I checked all the fences last week and everything's up to snuff. There's some native pasture down in the breaks in the south end, but the rest of it's in Bermuda and rye grass. There are some real good hay meadows, too, but they're not irrigated so you're lucky to get two cuttings most years."

When the tour was over, we thanked Roy and went back to the pickup. On the way out, I said, "I think that's a pretty nice place, but I've never bought property in my life. What do we do now?"

"Well, if you want to, you can make an offer, and we'll see if the sellers will take it. If they don't, they'll probably counter-offer, and then you can say yes or no to that. Where do you do your banking?"

"I opened an account at First American Commercial just this morning. They seemed real happy to take my money."

"I'll bet they did. Why don't we go back to my office and do some paperwork? I'll be happy to buy you some dinner afterwards."

"It's way past noon, so I reckon what you call dinner is supper to me, and I'll just take you up on that. Looking at property makes a man kind of hungry."

CHAPTER SIX

At his office, Miles called and left a message and his cell-phone number with Mrs., soon to be Ms, Hardcastle about my offer of one million dollars for the property, and then we went to Chico's for a good chicken-fried steak, and I was pleasantly full when Miles dropped me off at the Hilton. "I'll let you know as soon as I hear from the Hardcastles, Joe," he said on parting.

"Thanks, Miles," I replied and went on into the hotel. There were several people sitting in chairs in the lobby watching the door as I came through, and they all jumped to their feet at the same time. Someone turned on bright spotlights and aimed a TV camera at me. *Reporters.* All of them began to shout at once, but I kept right on going to the elevators, smiling but making no comment. One of the women was holding onto my jacket from behind and shouting into my ear, but I pulled away as the doors slid open, and with the help of a security guard I managed to get the doors to close while the big man held the crowd at bay.

When I arrived on the seventh floor I discovered that one reporter had been more enterprising than the others. A young woman with soft blond hair and flashing brown eyes was leaning on the wall next to the door to my suite. She was very pretty, and dressed in stylish clothes: a short girl, probably no more than five-four, and slender with a good figure. She looked much better than the shabby crowd in the lobby, and her manner was certainly more polite. "Mr. Garth," she began with a lovely smile, "I know you probably don't like this invasion of your space, but if you will just answer a few question for me, I'll be gone in a flash." It was not really a novel approach, but I had a hunch she had found it usually worked with men. The fact that she was attractive and her voice was low added to the feminine impression she cultivated.

I stopped and looked at her, smiling. "What's your name?"

"Lilly Walker," she replied. "I work for the Wichita Falls News, and I write a column, as well as feature stories in the Sunday edition of the paper."

"Well, Lilly, since you've taken the trouble to come up here, I might as well answer your questions. Come on in." I unlocked and opened the door to the suite, and then stood back to let Ms Walker enter first.

The door opened to a compact but well-appointed living/

sitting room, and I motioned to a chair. "Would you like a cup of coffee or something?"

"No, thanks. If you don't mind I'd like to record our conversation. It makes it easier for me when I write up the story." I nodded, and sat in a chair facing the reporter. She had very nice legs, and I liked the view from where I was sitting.

"My first question is the one everyone else will want to ask: what do you intend to do with all the money you've won?"

I laughed. "Lilly, I've been a working cowboy since I was fourteen, and the most money I've ever had was for an hour or two on payday. Depends on how long it takes to get to town. I don't know much about managing money, but I have some bankers who are helping me with that. Right now I'm still trying to get used to the idea that I no longer have to make my living on the back of a horse."

"So you haven't made any plans for the money yet?"

"If I have, I certainly wouldn't tell a reporter what they are. After the session I had in Austin with your colleagues, and that bunch of poor feeders down in the lobby, I have a hunch the best thing to say to you is nothing."

Lilly smiled, and dimples appeared in her smooth cheeks. The dimples were disarming, and I could tell she hoped they would get me to reveal something more about myself. Though I certainly enjoyed watching her flirt with me, revealing anything important wasn't going to happen.

"Are you married, Mr. Garth?"

"No."

"Ex-wives?"

"No."

"Girlfriends?"

"None."

"How did you feel when you learned that you had won the lottery?"

I laughed. "I felt like I was dreaming. Couldn't believe it at first, and then it seemed to be true, but I'm still pinching myself at times to see if this is really me."

"How much did you end up with after taxes?"

"Enough to pay for this hotel suite for a few days."

My short answers didn't please the journalist in Ms Walker at all, and she began to show some impatience. "Really, Mr. Garth, you could help me out by giving me some better answers."

"Really, Ms Walker," I mimicked her tone, "I don't want you or anyone else prying into my private life." I stood and motioned for her to do the same. "Thanks for stopping by, Ms Walker, but I believe our little talk is over."

Lilly stood and turned toward the door that I was holding open. "You're making a mistake, Mr. Garth. If you give me some information so I can write a feature on you, you'll soon be old news, and the other reporters will leave you alone. If you don't, you never know what people might write about you."

"Ms Walker, just because I'm a cowboy doesn't mean that I'm also a fool. I'll admit I don't know a lot about reporters or newspapers, but I do know that if anyone prints lies or made-up stories about me, I have enough money to hire a good lawyer to bring a lawsuit against that reporter and newspaper. And I know that you didn't turn the tape recorder off and you're hoping I'll let something slip. It isn't going to happen, girl."

Lilly's face stiffened, and I could see her shift gears, as if she suddenly knew that I was right, and she *had* assumed that I was stupid. Looking up at me I think she really saw me for the first time. Now, I'm no heartthrob, but I'm not ugly either. I'm six-one, my hair is brown and my eyes are blue, and I was once told by a girl that I'm what's called "ruggedly handsome," whatever that means. I smiled as I looked down into her pretty face, but I still ushered her out and closed the door behind her.

After I closed the door I called the front desk and asked to speak with the person in charge. An assistant manager came on the line, and I told her about my unwanted guest. "Now, how would she know my room number? Did one of your employees tell her, perhaps for a few bucks? I'd appreciate it if you would find out. I'm not necessarily trying to hide, you understand, but

I don't want to come in and find reporters and other strangers camped at my door."

The assistant manager remembered what the manager had told her: Joe Garth was a celebrity, and as such he was entitled to be protected from the public. His suite was private, and no one was to be allowed on the 7th floor without his approval. "I'm sorry, Mr. Garth. I assure you that we will find out who is responsible and that person will be fired."

"Well, now, let's hold on a minute. I don't really want to see someone put out on the street over this. Why don't you find out who it was and send him or her up to see me. I think a little kindness will do a better job than a whole lot of pain. And put the word around that *I'll* pay your people to keep this from happening again."

"All right, Mr. Garth. I'll do whatever you think is right."

I put the phone down and it rang again almost at once. "Hello," I said.

"Joe, this is Miles. It looks like you've just bought yourself a ranch. I've talked to both Mr. and Mrs. Hardcastle, and they're willing to sign on the dotted line. I'll put some paperwork together, and we can meet at your bank in the morning, if that's all right with you."

"Well, I don't have anything else going on tomorrow, so what time do you want to meet?"

"Let's say 10:00 a.m. That'll give the bankers a chance to get the sleep out of their eyes." I wondered if the two bankers I had met ever slept in their quest for money, but I didn't say so. I agreed on the time and hung up the phone.

In a few minutes there was a knock at the door, and when I opened it, a sheepish looking bellhop was standing there. "Mr. Garth, my name's Sean Charles, and I apologize for telling that reporter your room number."

"Come in and let's talk about it," I replied. "How much did she pay you, Sean?"

The young man pulled a ten-dollar bill out of his pocket and silently held it out. I took it, and said, "Sean, I'm not really a celebrity. I got lucky with a lottery ticket and won a bunch of money, and some people think that makes me a movie star, but I know better. I'm really a lot like you; I've always worked hard for my money, and I've never made much, so I know how it is when a windfall comes my way. I do like some privacy, though, and I don't want anyone to come up here unless I invite them. So here's what I'll do." I laid Sean's ten on the table, pulled a wad of cash out of my pocket, peeled a ten-dollar bill off the roll and laid it on top of the one on the table.

"I'll match what the reporter gave you, and there will be more if you and your friends see to it that I'm not disturbed up here. Now, I'm not going to be in the hotel much longer, so when I leave there will be a large tip for you and anyone else who has helped me in any way. I would appreciate it if you would pass that word around." I picked up the two tens and handed them to the young bellhop.

"Thanks, Mr. Garth," Sean said with a large smile on his face. "I figured you were going to chew me out and keep the money the lady gave me. I never expected you to be this nice. Don't you worry, I'll pass the word, and you won't be disturbed again."

I stood and held the door open. "Good. I know I can count on you, Sean."

The beaming young man left, and I settled down to an evening of mindless TV. Since I was not used to late hours, by 9:30 I was showered and ready for bed when the phone rang. "Mr. Garth? This is Lilly Walker. I am calling to apologize for my rudeness earlier this evening. I'm afraid we reporters don't often think about the privacy of our subjects. I won't bother you again."

This was a new direction, and I had a hunch that at this point I was supposed to forgive her and ask her to go out with me. "Why, thanks for the apology, Ms Walker. I appreciate it."

Silence on the phone. "Well, uh, I guess that's all," she said with a hopeful note in her voice.

"Goodbye, Ms Walker."

The girl *was* very attractive, but she was also a purebred reporter, and even an innocent comment by me could, and probably would, be blown up into an expose.

The next morning when I arrived at the bank, I was immediately recognized and Mr. Wilkins came right out to greet me. As we were talking, Miles Moore arrived, and, after introductions, we were both led to the elevator, which whisked us up to the inner sanctum. Mr. Argus was all smiles as he greeted us, and after offering coffee and pastry, he asked, "What can I do for you this morning, Mr. Garth?"

"Well, Miles has shown me a nice ranch, and the offer I made was accepted, so I guess I want to transfer some money so the deal can be finalized."

"No problem, Mr. Garth. No problem at all. How much did you have in mind?"

"Let's see, I wrote a check for $20,000 for earnest money, so I guess I'll need nine hundred and eighty thousand for the rest, plus whatever the closing costs are. Miles here can give you the numbers."

Argus gulped, and his face changed. "Well now, Mr. Garth, I think we can take care of that, but I have a suggestion to make. Why don't you use ten percent of your money, and borrow the rest from the bank? We'd be happy to make you a thirty-year real estate loan for $900,000.00, and you could let your money continue to work for you."

I thought about that. Taking the whole million from my account might not be the best way to do things. "What interest rate would you charge me, Mr. Argus?"

The banker was caught in his own net. When I opened the account Argus had assured me that if I wanted to borrow money from the bank, I would be offered a low 5% interest. I grinned inside as I watched the banker struggle. "Well, Mr. Garth, you're earning 4% on your account right now, and as I told you yesterday, the loan interest would normally be 5%, but I think we'll just make the interest amounts the same. What about a four percent loan? That means that the interest on the loan will be more than covered by the interest your account is earning. And the interest rate on your account will probably go up, but the loan rate will remain the same." It also meant that my money wouldn't leave the bank, but Argus didn't seem to feel the need to point that out.

"Sounds like I can't lose, Mr. Argus," I replied. "Let's do it that way."

"Fine, Mr. Garth. Do you want to add taxes and insurance to your loan? That means you only make one payment a month."

"Okay, let's add those too. How much will the monthly payment be?"

Argus did some quick calculating. "The loan payment itself will be $4,296.73. I don't know the exact amount for taxes and insurance, but those two should be about another $2,000.00 a month. Let's say about $6,000.00 a month. When we have all the actual figures, do you want us to just debit your account every month for the payment? That'll save you having to write a check."

"Sounds good, Mr. Argus. I don't much like paperwork, so any way you can relieve me of it will be welcome." This did seem like the easiest way to do things, but I wondered if it was the best way? Maybe I needed to see a money advisor, if there was such a thing. I glanced at Miles, but he was looking down, inspecting the toes of his boots. Should I ask his advice? Maybe not. Might put him on the spot.

Argus called a loan officer to come to his office and bring the necessary paperwork, and I signed my name on several pieces of paper without looking at them. After all, a banker wouldn't try to take advantage of someone with millions in his bank, would he?

When we left the bank, I asked, "When can I move in, Miles?"

"Well, all the paperwork should be finished by the end of the week. I think you can take possession any time after that.

Shall we say a week from today?"

"Sounds good to me, Miles. I reckon once I get settled I'll have a house warming. If I invited you and your wife, would you come?"

"We'd be happy to, Joe. Just let me know when."

I went back to the hotel feeling good. I now owned a ranch, and I would soon be doing cowboy work again, only this time I'd be the boss, and I figured to pay myself more than $900.00 a month.

CHAPTER SEVEN

The first day on my new ranch dawned sunny and cold. Winter was coming, just as the early blue norther of a couple weeks before foretold. Miles had suggested that I meet him at the ranch about 9:00 a.m. and he had given me the gate code, but the cowboy in me wouldn't let me sleep past daylight, so I was having breakfast in a nearby greasy spoon long before the appointed hour. With my belly full of hotcakes and eggs, I climbed back into the pickup and headed east down U.S. 287.

The sun was well up when I parked in front of the house and followed the paved walk around the side of the building and down toward the stables. I was going to go get Buck the next day, and I wanted to see if there was any hay or feed for him. When I entered the long stable building, Roy Alcorn was just coming out of the bunkhouse. "Mornin', Mr. Garth," he said.

"Mornin' Roy. I guess you heard that I bought this place."

"Yep, I sure did. Am I fired, or do I get to stay on?"

"Oh, I reckon an old busted up bronc stomper like you couldn't get a job anywhere else, and I'd sure hate to have to turn you out to the county trough, so I guess I might as well keep you on," I said with a grin.

Roy was opened-mouthed until he saw that I was only fooling. "Oh, don't let my age and infirmities bother you, Mr. Millionaire! If you want to fire me, go ahead. I'll just run to the newspapers and tell 'em what a sorry rascal you are, firin' an old man on your first day on the ranch." Alcorn had a twinkle in his eye, and I could see that we would get on fine.

"Well, I guess I'll *have* to keep you on then. I've had my fill of newspaper reporters for a while. How are we fixed for hay and horse feed? I've got a good cow horse I want to bring over from the Slash T."

For answer, Roy led me down the alleyway to the far end of the building. A special section had been built into the barn to hold several hundred square bales of hay, and it was about half full. "Plenty of hay, and right here's the feed room." The cowboy pulled a door open and turned on a light. There were several bags of feed stacked in the room, along with metal bins for bulk feed and racks for salt blocks.

"Looks good," Joe said. "Tomorrow we'll take a little trip out to the Slash T and bring Buck back with us."

We went on to the large hay barn with cattle feeders all

along the south side. It too held some square bales of hay, and outside under a metal roof was a long triple row of large round bales. "There's an old tractor still here, and when we had cows I used to feed them these round bales of Coastal. Got to tell you, though, the tractor's too small, and it's about shot. We need a new one with more horsepower."

"Tell you what, Roy. You make up a list of things we need for horses and cows and the ranch in general and I'll go over it. Later in the week we'll go to town and do a little shopping. Then next week, I want to buy some mama cows and a couple of good bulls. This place is crying for livestock."

We were in the middle of a discussion about the best cattle breeds when Miles found us. "Just as I figured," he said. "You couldn't wait to get out here, could you?"

"Nope, and I reckon it's a good thing I came early. Roy's been left alone here so long, he's taken to sleepin' 'til noon." Roy gave a shout and threw his hat to the ground in mock anger. Miles laughed, and we headed up to the house.

My move from the hotel to the ranch later in the day went as smooth as glass. My few personal items were quickly loaded in the pickup, and, as promised, I left a generous tip – $500.00 – to be split by all the bellhops and desk clerks.

Since the house came furnished with everything but the bed in the master suite, I had ordered a bed to be sent out from the Continental Furniture Mart, and it arrived just as I did. By nightfall, I had a nice fire going in the den, and Roy and I were seated in comfortable chairs on each side of it as we talked about my plans for the ranch.

The next morning Roy came up to the house for breakfast. Neither of us were good cooks, but we managed to fry some eggs and bacon from the groceries I'd had brought when I moved in.

"Roy," I said around a mouthful of overdone eggs, "I think I need a cook. There are servants' quarters in this house, so maybe I need a housekeeper, too, or one person who does both. That is unless you want to come up here and clean the house everyday, make my bed, and like that."

"Not only do I *not* want to be your nursemaid, I'd like to have one of my own. I'm thinkin' about a twenty-five-year-old, blond, built like a..."

"That'll do," I said. "I'm talking about a housekeeper and cook for the big house, not the bunkhouse."

We were still bantering about servants when we climbed into the pickup and headed off to the Slash T.

When we arrived at the ranch, I went right to the foreman's office. Matt was there, and he welcomed me like a long lost brother. "Garth! Good to see you, man. Did you spend all your money and come back to get your old job? I can use you, but, of course, you'd have to take a pay cut. Can't pay top money to a green hand, you know."

I grinned and shook Matt's hand hard, pleased to see my former boss. "Actually, Mr. Walters, I came back to see if I could hire you. I need a full-time housekeeper and cook, and I figure since you've been my nanny for so long, you'd fill both position hands down." Matt told me in no uncertain terms to find another nanny someplace else. I went on to tell Matt about the ranch I'd bought, and he promised to come out and see it first chance he got.

Roy had followed me into the office, and I introduced him. "I want to pick up Buck and my gear, Matt. Do I owe you anything for storage?"

"Nope, not a thing. That's a mighty good horse, and if you don't want him, I'd be happy to make you an offer."

"Sorry, Matt. He's the best horse I've ever owned, and he's not for sale. Before we load up, though, I'd like to say goodbye to Handy, if you don't mind."

Matt nodded his head. "Sure, sure. You two go back a long ways. And don't be a stranger, Joe. You come see us poor folks from time to time."

Handy and Jose were both in the kitchen, and Roy and I had a cup of coffee with them. Handy promised to come see the new ranch and bring Jose along as soon as possible. He also said that he'd miss seeing my "ugly mug" every day.

It didn't take long to hook the trailer up and load Buck. In fact, he was so happy to see me that when I pointed at the trailer, he loaded himself. After throwing my saddle and gear in the back of the truck, we were ready to go. Handy and Jose waved us off.

"Looks like it was a pretty good place to work, Joe," Roy said.

"One of the best outfits I've ever worked for," I replied. "I'll miss some things about it, but with winter comin' on, I don't think I'll miss the long cold rides and workin' cows out of bog holes."

I had been feeling pretty good about escaping the news-hounds until we came to the gate to the ranch. Parked along the road on both sides were cars and TV vans. Several people with cameras of one sort or another were standing in the road and leaning on the closed gate. As I pulled in toward the gate, a shaggy looking young man jumped in front of the pickup.

"Oh, no," I moaned. "How did they find out where I moved to? I didn't tell anyone."

"No, but the sale was recorded at the courthouse, and that means that now everybody in the county knows," Roy said.

Though we locked the doors and rolled the windows up tight, people were pounding on the fenders and trying to pull the doors open. They were also hanging on the trailer and spooking Buck, and I could feel him shifting back and forth. "Well, I might just as well get out," I said in resignation. "Once I'm out, you lock the door and open the gate. Pull right on through and don't stop. Take Buck down and unload him. I'll walk down when I've gotten rid of these vultures."

I eased out of the pickup and pushed my way back to the trailer. A man and a woman were trying to get the back trailer gate open, but I stopped them with a shout. The crowd quieted for a minute, and I backed away from the trailer as Roy pulled it forward. "Listen to me!" I yelled. "Shut up and listen!" The crowd slowly grew quiet.

"I don't know how you found this place, but I want to make it clear that anyone who climbs the fence or crawls over the gate without my permission will be arrested and prosecuted for trespassing. Now, I'll give an interview and answer a few questions, and then I'd appreciate it if you'd all trail off and find someone else to pester." Looking over the pack, I spotted Lily Walker behind the crowd looking cool and composed. "Ms Walker, if you'll come up here I'd like you to do the interview." She gave me a small smile and moved through the crowd.

"Now, all of you listen up and you can share what I'm going to say. You TV people go ahead and set up." A man came forward and clipped two small microphones to my shirt, and the cameraman turned on his bright lights, even though it was a sunny day.

Lilly waited until everything was ready, and then said, "Mr. Garth, I understand you bought this ranch with the money you won in the lottery, is that correct?"

"Well, Ms Walker, I sure couldn't afford it on cowboy pay."

"Do you plan to raise cattle here?"

"Yes, cattle and horses."

"And was that a new horse that was in the trailer?"

"No, that was a horse I've owned for several years. He's a good cow horse."

The interview went on for some minutes, but much to my surprise, Lilly didn't ask any of the prying questions I expected. However, as soon as I said I would take some questions from the rest of the reporters, the coyotes came out. "Where's your wife, Garth?" "Have you got a girlfriend, Joe, or a boyfriend?" "Will you be having wild parties out here?" "How much, money do you have left now that you bought this place?" "Don't you know that slaughtering animals for food is the same as murdering helpless people?" (This from a rabid animal rights advocate wearing a wide leather belt.) "Since you're not married, are you gay?"

I didn't answer any of those questions; I just held up my hands in disgust and said, "That's enough. You people need to get a life of your own instead of harassing folks like me. No more questions," and I pushed my way through the still shouting newsies and toward the closed gate. A quiet voice beside me said, "Thanks for the interview, Mr. Garth."

I stopped and looked back to see that Lilly Walker had followed me through the crowd, and I grinned at her. "You're welcome, Ms Walker. If you'll come back after this crowd's gone, I'd like to talk to you. Just speak your name into the box over there and the gate will open."

I didn't wait for a reply; I just climbed over the gate and walked on down toward the buildings. I could have opened the gate, but I figured if I did at least some of the pack of newshounds were prepared to follow me through.

The first thing I did when he got back to the house was program the gate opener by entering Lilly Walker's name. The next thing was to go see if Buck was all right.

Roy had unloaded the horse and turned him out into a large pen behind the horse barn, and he'd filled the rack with hay, which Buck was enjoying. I whistled and Buck nickered and came to the fence so I could pat him on the neck. "Good to have you around again, Buck," I said.

"Roy, I'd appreciate it if you'd unhitch the trailer. I'm going up to the house because I'm going to have a guest there pretty soon. That means you'll have to get your own meal, and I know you'll miss my cooking."

"Actually, I appreciate the fact that you're *not* going to cook for me again. I'll take care of the trailer. You want the pickup in front of the house or in the garage?"

"Neither, just leave it down here."

When I went through the back door, the bell was ringing at the front. Ms Walker hadn't wasted any time.

"You don't think much of reporters, do you, Mr. Garth?"

"Probably even less than you think of cowboys, Ms Walker."

That brought a laugh, and the pretty face lit up. "Touché," she said.

I invited her to sit down and put on some coffee, for the sky had clouded over, and the warm day was turning into a chilly evening. When I came back into the den, I sat down facing her. "I appreciate the way you handled the interview, Ms Walker. Do you think it will get the news people off my back for a while?"

"I think so. They learned that you guard your words too closely to be newsworthy. However, this house and all of the buildings can be seen clearly from the road, so I have a hunch there will be photographers up there taking pictures for several days yet."

"Just what are they looking for, Lilly? I assume I can call you Lilly."

"Sure, if you'll let me call you Joe. This 'Mr. and Ms' business gets kind of tiresome, doesn't it?" At my nod she continued. "They're looking for something to take to their editors, like catching you beating a horse or chasing naked girls around the pastures. Scandal sells; kindness doesn't."

"Oh, well, that's no problem. I don't intend to beat my horse, and there are no naked girls around, or any other kind of girls, for that matter. Now, tell me about yourself, Lilly. You don't seem like the run-of-mill nosey reporter, and yet you did show up with that crowd today."

Lilly smiled, and the dimples showed. "I *am* a reporter, Joe, and you should never forget it. But I'm not a sleaze reporter like some of those that waited for you. And because I'm not that kind of reporter, I'll probably never win a Pulitzer."

I chuckled and said, "I'll tell you what I'll do, Lilly. In a few days you call me and I'll give you an exclusive interview. I'll even answer some questions about myself, as long as they're not too nosey. You can bring a photographer along if you think it's worthwhile. How about it?"

"You're talking about a feature, and I think my editor will go for that, Joe. And thanks, but why?"

"Let's just say I'm a sucker for a pretty face. Now, I have a question for you. Where can I find a housekeeper who can cook?

The best I can do is fry eggs, as Roy will confirm, and I can't do that very well, and I hate cleaning, but I've never hired a housekeeper and I don't know the first thing about it."

Lilly laughed. "Joe, don't you know that when you have a lot of money you are supposed to know everything? And even if you don't, you're supposed to *act* like you do. Anyway, why don't you call an employment agency and ask them to send out some housekeeper candidates? I assume you want a live-in domestic, do you have quarters for such a person?"

"Oh, I've got the quarters, all right. Do you want to see them?" Lilly nodded and we went into the kitchen and through a door on the north side.

"This hallway goes on out to the garage," I said opening a door set midway down the hall. We entered the spacious living room of a small apartment. There was a kitchen, a bathroom, and a bedroom, and all of them were very well appointed and comfortable.

"This is a very nice apartment," Lilly said. "And it's very clean, too. Maybe you need to get whoever cleaned these rooms to be your housekeeper."

We went out to the empty four-car garage, and then back into the house. As we took our seats again Lilly said, "So, if you're not going to tell me any secrets tonight, why did you ask me to come to your home? I got the impression that you don't really want reporters around."

"Oh, that's easy. I thought I'd ask you out to dinner, and if tonight's not good, you name a time. My social calendar is pretty much open right now."

Lilly laughed, a throaty chuckle that made me smile. "You really are naïve, Joe. If we went out to dinner tonight, that would be news, and you'd be followed home again. There's not a restaurant in town that doesn't have a waiter, usually a headwaiter, who provides information to some reporter. If I do agree to go to dinner with you it will be long after you are no longer news."

"Well, at least you didn't give me an absolute 'no.' How

about calling me when I'm no longer news and letting me know when it will be all right to ask you to dinner?"

The laugh came again, and on this note, Lilly left to go back to reporting.

Since my bid for a supper companion didn't pan out, I went to the kitchen and made myself a bologna sandwich, and took it back to the den to eat. I still needed a housekeeper, so I pulled out the phone book to see what I could find. The problem was, I didn't really know where to start, but something Lilly said had stayed with me. I began looking under "Domestics," but all I found were references to stores that sold towels and things. Oh well, that'd have to wait.

Putting on a heavy jacket, I went out to the stables to check on Buck. Tomorrow I figured he and I would take a closer look at the ranch.

CHAPTER EIGHT

Things settled down as the days rolled into fall. I trimmed down Roy's list a bit, but we did go supply shopping and bought a new John Deere tractor with a full set of equipment, as well as many other things needed for the ranch. When it came time to pay, I just wrote checks for everything, not very concerned about what my balance was.

Since I'd never had a checking account, I hadn't a clue as to how to balance a checkbook, so when the bank statement came I would just go to the bank and have one of the girls balance it for me. It seemed like whenever I showed up at the bank, someone called the president and he made an appearance. Mr. Argus usually invited me to lunch or dinner, but I always declined. The banker was friendly enough on the surface, but other than the money I had in his bank, I didn't think we had much in common, and I often had the feeling that the little man was looking down on me.

After several days of interviewing cook/housekeepers, one finally emerged from the pack that seemed right for the job. She was not blond, twenty-five and well built as per Roy's request, but she sure knew her way around the kitchen.

I had asked all of the candidates to fix a meal, and Roy and I had eaten them. Mrs. Blanco fixed Mexican food: Spanish rice, refried beans, beef and chicken enchiladas, and stacks of homemade flour tortillas. At the end of the meal, I hired her on the spot and called the employment agency to tell them I wouldn't need any more candidates.

Rita Blanco was a widow with a large brood of grown children, and an even larger flock of grandchildren. She was happy, meticulously clean, energetic and a comfort to have around the house. Rita was short and overweight, but she was very light on her feet, moving swiftly from task to task. She soon had the household running like a well-oiled machine.

On the day the forty head of registered Black Angus cows and two bulls arrived, Lilly followed them through the gate to do the interview I had promised her. It was a cold morning with occasional sleet blowing from the north. As arranged, Roy and I met the cattle trucks at the barns, and Lilly was ushered into the house for hot coffee by Mrs. Blanco.

I had bought the cattle at a dispersal sale, and while I didn't know the man who'd sold them, he obviously knew cattle for the small herd had been well taken care of. They were expensive; each cow cost $2,000.00, and the bulls were $3,000.00 a piece. But the cows were all bred and would calve in the spring, and I knew that in a few years I would have the herd I wanted.

Once the cattle were settled in, I left Roy in charge and went up to the house. As I came in the back door I heard the two women laughing and speaking fast Spanish. I shrugged out of my coat, hung my hat on a peg, and went on into the den. "Oh, Mr. Garth," Rita said. "Your friend and I have been having the good talk. Sit down, and I'll bring fresh coffee," and she bustled off to the kitchen.

I took Lilly's outstretched hand, perhaps holding it a little too long, and grinned at her. "I see you've been getting acquainted with the Jewel of the Rafter JG."

"She's terrific. If I could afford a housekeeper, I would try to hire her away from you."

"Wait until you taste her food. Rita is the best cook in ten counties, maybe in the whole state of Texas. You will stay for lunch, won't you?"

"Love to, as long as we can have the feature done by noon. The photographer is coming at one, and I can only have him until three."

I nodded. "No problem. You saw the trucks full of cattle as

you came in. I want to have some pictures of them to go in the newspaper. That's free advertising, and ranchers will know that I'll have registered calves for sale soon."

"You're learning, Joe," she said, showing the dimples. She pulled out her tape recorder and placed it on the table, and then said, "Let's get started. It's been two months since you won the lottery; how has your life changed in that time?"

Rita brought coffee in and quietly sat her tray down. We both thanked her, and went back to the interview. At 10:30 we took a break and I led her down to the barns to see the new cattle. The sleet had stopped, but the day was still cold.

Lilly looked and acted like a city girl, but she asked good questions about barns and livestock. I wondered about that, but I made no comment. "How about horses, Joe?" she asked. "The last time I was here you only had one, but now I see several over there by the other barn."

We walked over that way, and Buck came to the fence to say hello. "I don't have any breeding stock yet, Lilly, but I did pick up some good cow ponies at an estate sale. When we work the cattle and then turn them out, Roy and I will be using these horses. After the first of the year I'll be going to some breeder's sales. I want a good Quarter Horse stallion and five or six quality mares."

"Will Roy be able to handle all of these animals?" Lilly asked with a twinkle in her eye.

Roy had tagged along from the cattle pens, and he snorted. "No he won't, Miss Walker, and I'm glad you brought that up. Do I get some help, Mr. Joe?"

I laughed at him. "Why, you lazy old coot. It'll do you good to have to work for a change. You've put away so much of Rita's good cookin' that you're gettin' a roll around your middle."

"Well, I for sure wasn't gainin' any weight when I was eating *your* cooking," Roy replied.

Lilly laughed at us. "You two almost sound like a married couple. Do you always bicker like this?"

"Roy just doesn't have any respect for the boss," I said. "I have a hunch that's why he had to take this job. His reputation's too bad to get hired on a real workin' ranch."

Roy sputtered, but he was grinning when we left him to go back to the house.

Once we were seated again, Rita came in with iced tea and let me know that lunch would be served at 11:30, leaving plenty of time to eat before the photographer came.

In fact, lunch was over and we were still seated at the table visiting and drinking Rita's good coffee when the photographer called down from the gate. Rita pushed the control to let him in, and Lilly went out to meet him.

In two hours the photos were completed, and the photographer was driving back up the driveway. I led Lilly out of the cold and back into the den to stand before the warm log fire and asked, "Is it okay to ask you to dinner now, Lilly? Do you think your colleagues will leave us alone?"

She smiled and dimpled, suddenly almost shy. "I think it will be all right, Joe. I was kind of hoping you'd ask."

"Then how about dinner tonight? I really like catfish, and I've been told that Uncle Lynn's is the best catfish place in town and it's right on your way back to Wichita Falls."

Lilly agreed, and she stayed in the den drinking coffee and talking to Rita, who was secretly trying to do some not-so-subtle matchmaking, while I went out to help Roy with feeding.

When we had hayed the cows and fed the horses, I said, "Roy, how many full time men do you think you'll need? Keep in mind that we're going to have horses here after the first of the year."

"Right now I won't need more than one, and he doesn't have to know much. Feeding's going to take some time, that and cleaning the manure out of the cow and horse barns. There's some paintin' that needs done, too. What I need more than anything is a ranch hand rather than a cowboy. When you get the horses, then I'll need a cowboy who can help me. I've worked on a stud farm, so I can handle the breeding, but we may need a man to break some young stock and watch the cows."

I thought for a minute. "I think I know where I can get a ranch hand, and a good one, too, if the Slash T will let me have him. Course, this means the bunkhouse kitchen will be put into use, so we'll have to have a cook, and I'll look for one of those, too. Once we have the horses, then we'll hire a cowboy.

"Now, this is Tuesday, and Thursday I want to brand and vaccinate the cattle so we can turn them out on the weekend. We'll need a couple of part time hands for that. You got any ideas?"

Roy thought for a minute. "I know a couple of men who cowboy part time. One of them's an accountant, and the other's a schoolteacher, but they like to do cowboy work. How much you payin'?"

"We only need them for one day since we don't have many head to work, and we've sure got good chutes to use. What about $50.00 each for the day?"

"Fifty? Why, you only pay me $1,000.00 a month, and you're going to give two dudes $50.00 for one day's work? I think that's a way too much!"

I grinned at the old cowboy. "Why Roy, I didn't think you cared anything about money. And anyway, you get medical insurance and retirement, your food and housing's free, and I furnish the horses. I reckon you're overpaid." I held up my hand to stop Roy's budding protest. "But, just to stop your whining, I'll give you a fifty dollar bonus for the day so you'll be paid the same as the townies. Will that smooth your ruffled feathers?"

"I reckon it will, at least for a while. Okay, I'll call the two men. The accountant works for himself, so I doubt he'll have much problem getting off, but I don't know about the teacher. Anyway, leave it to me and I'll have two hands here early Thursday morning."

Dinner at Uncle Lynn's was a success from my point of view, and from Lilly's too, judging by her pleased look. She had followed me in her car since she was going back to her apartment after dinner, so when the meal was over we said our goodbyes in the parking lot. "It's been a fun day, Joe," she said standing close inside the circle of my arms and looking up at me. "Thanks for the feature. You'll be in next Sunday's paper, so be sure and read about yourself."

"Lilly, I've enjoyed having you around today. I hope you'll come often and stay late."

She laughed, and then let the dimples appear, and I leaned down and kissed her. It was a good kiss, but not a passionate one – not yet. Still, when I watched her leave, I experienced a twinge of loss.

I climbed into my old pickup and headed back to the ranch with a smile pulling at the corners of his mouth. For a cynical reporter, Ms Lilly Walker sure made a nice armful.

CHAPTER NINE

While Roy was finding help for Thursday's cattle work, I called the Slash T and talked to Matt Walters. "Matt, I'd like to try and hire a couple of men away from you, but I thought I'd better let you know before I strike. I need a ranch hand, and I've always liked young Tom Hansen. Seems to be a hard worker, and I know he wants to be a cowboy. How about if I offer him a job?"

Walters was always protective of his men, even though he knew that most of them were transitory. Cowboys had a way of leaving from time to time to see if the grass was greener somewhere else. But he also liked Tom Hansen, and he knew the boy would have a better deal as the only hand on my place than as one of a bunch at the Slash T. "Okay, Joe. I like the boy too, so if he goes to work for you, you better treat him right."

"No problem, Matt. He'll think he's died and gone to heaven when he gets away from you." Walters chuckled.

"Now, this next one may not make you so happy, Matt. I want to offer Handy a job as cook here. What do you think?"

"Not Handy! That man can really put food on the table, and you know how hard it is to find a good cook for the men, I mean one who can fix things the way they like 'em. No, Joe, please don't ask Handy. I don't want to lose him."

"Well, I do understand, Matt, but what if he asks me? You know we're friends from who flung the chunk."

"If he asks you, I guess you can make him an offer, but I'd sure hate to lose him."

I was quiet for a bit. I'd known all along that I was not going to ask Handy because the cook and I'd been friends too long, and an old friend as a boss or an employee seldom worked out. I only said what I did to soften Matt up. "Okay then, how about Jose Alvarez? Handy's taught him how to fix good grub, and it would almost be like having the man himself."

"Sure, Joe, you can ask Jose. He's young and Handy's taught him well. Go ahead. You have my blessing on that one." There was relief in Matt's voice.

"Okay, Matt, that's what I'll do. I'll call the cookhouse now, and try to reach Tom tonight after work, if that's all right with you."

"Fine, Joe. Good to talk to you, but please leave the rest of my crew alone. You'll ruin them with that showplace of yours anyway, and good ranch hands and cowboys are hard enough to find as it is." When I hung up I wondered how long it would be before Matt figured out how I'd snookered him.

I talked to both Jose and Tom, and hired them for more than they were presently getting. I also talked to my friend Handy, who chewed me out over taking Jose, but settled down when I told him how nice the bunkhouse kitchen was. "Okay, rich man," he finally said. "But if everything's so great, why didn't you ask for me, your old buddy, instead of Jose?"

"Well, I did think of it, but what with your aches and pains and your age, I figured I needed a younger man, one that would be with me for awhile." I put the phone down while Handy was still sputtering.

Jose had an old car so there was no need to pick the two new hands up at the Slash T, and by Wednesday night they were settled in.

Thursday was bright and sunny, cool but not cold. It was early December, and the weather was always kind of iffy at this time of year, but it looked like we would have a nice day for working cattle.

The two part-time hands arrived together in one vehicle, and they were happy to be away from their normal jobs for a day, and ready to cowboy. Roy had a couple of horses saddled for them, and the five of us – including Tom – went into the large pasture and began to move the cattle down to the working pens. These cattle were not like the range cows found on the big ranches. They were used to being handled, and they were quickly penned in a big holding corral. As the last cowboy came through, Tom Hansen closed the gate behind him.

Whoever had designed the pens and chutes had known about cattle. The large pen where all of the cattle were held narrowed down at one end with a gate that led into an approach chute. From this chute the cattle were moved down to the squeeze, a hydraulic chute that would squeeze big cattle into immobility, eliminating injuries to cattle or men, though, of course, the safety of the cattle was of primary importance.

I allotted the jobs: Roy would work the squeeze, Pete Reynolds, the teacher, and Tom would vaccinate and ear tag, I would brand, and the accountant, Arlis Knowles, would prod the cattle down the chute.

The work went smoothly, and by noon when Jose rang the triangle outside the bunkhouse kitchen, we were more than half done. I'd told Rita that I would not have lunch at the main house, and I ate with the rest of the men. While we were eating Jose's good steaks, Pete Reynolds asked, "Joe, since you won all that money, and you can afford to pay people to work for you, why are you helping with this project?"

I laughed and replied, "Do you like to teach, Pete?"

"Yes, I do."

"Well, I like to work with cows and horses. The difference is, a few weeks ago I *had* to do cowboy work to make a living, and there were times when I'd just as soon go fishin'. But now I can work or not as I please, and that makes the work more appealing. Do you understand?"

"I guess I do. If I won the lottery, I'd still want to teach, but I would pick my own time and school. Yeah, that makes sense."

We went back to work after a noon rest and finished by 4:00. I paid the extra help in my office up at the house, and when they were gone, I called my bookkeeper, the one who worked for the accountant Mr. Argus at the bank had recommended, and told her to put a bonus for Roy, Tom and Jose in their next pay-checks. Roy would get his fifty, and Tom and Jose would each get twenty-five.

On Saturday I had Tom saddle a horse for himself to help Roy and me push the cattle down into the south pasture. There was enough rough ground and shelter there along the creek that it was a good place to winter cattle. Tom was excited about being able to do more cowboy work, something that had rarely happened to him when he worked for the Slash T.

A cold north wind was blowing Sunday when I went into town to get a newspaper. Rita had Sundays off, and I took her in with me. She didn't have a car, in fact she didn't have a license, so usually one of her kids came out and picked her up on the weekends, but this would save them a trip.

On the way into town, Rita invited me to attend church with her. I had gone to church and Sunday school regularly when I was a boy, but since I left home at eighteen I had confined my religious duty to a few funerals and one wedding. Still, I didn't have to be anywhere special this morning, so I agreed, though I wondered aloud if I was dressed properly.

"Oh, your clothes are fine," Rita said. "A lot of the men wear jeans and boots at our church."

Because she was Hispanic, I assumed that Rita was Catholic, and I was surprised when she directed me to a medium-sized metal church building with a sign near the front that said, "Chapel of Grace."

When we entered the front doors Rita's large family was there waiting for her to appear, and after introductions, I was immediately included in the clan. We went on into a large, barn-like room that was obviously used as a gym during the week. Hundreds of chairs were placed in a large semi-circle in front of a platform. Rita's oldest son, Raul, introduced me to the pastor, a large middle-aged man with a smiling face. "Welcome, Mr. Garth," he said rather formally. "I hope you will enjoy worshipping with us."

"Thank you, Reverend Whiting. I'm sure I will."

There was a band on the platform with drums and guitars, as well as a piano and several other instruments, including a trumpet. I hadn't been in a lot of churches, but those I had been in usually had only a piano, with at most an organ to accompany it. I had never seen a set of drums or a trumpet in a church in my life, and I wondered what the service would be like.

As Rita's family took their seats, filling a long row of chairs, the band began to play and a young man stood on the platform to lead the singing. There were no hymnals, but there was a large screen on the wall behind the platform and the words of the song suddenly appeared there from a hidden projector.

The music was lively and pleasant, with some slow songs interspersed to make the whole thing seem more worshipful. All of the people stood to sing, and they sang for a good thirty minutes. I enjoyed the music, but standing on concrete for a long time wearing cowboy boots wasn't real comfortable.

Finally, the congregation was asked to sit down, and large baskets were placed on the floor in front of the platform. The pastor prayed, and then, while the band struck up a jazzy tune, everyone was invited to come down to the front and drop money into the baskets. I followed Rita and Raul, and dropped a twenty into a basket before following them back to their seats.

When the music was over, the pastor voiced a long prayer and then began to preach. He was really quite good. I had wondered, judging from the music, if he'd be a shouter like some I'd heard from time to time on TV, but he spoke in a conversational tone for the most part, and he was funny and straightforward. Plus, what he said made a lot of sense.

The service finally ended, and I said my goodbyes to Rita and her family and went on my way. The pastor had shaken my hand at the door and invited me back. Nice guy, and I really liked the way he handled himself. I decided that I probably needed to go to church more often, and if I actually enjoyed it, so much the better.

Not far from the church there was a newspaper rack, and

when I had my paper, I headed back to the ranch.

Lilly had done a great job on the feature. There were several pictures of me and the horses and cattle, and she had stuck to the facts without trying to sensationalize the lottery winning or my lifestyle. I felt good about the story, and as soon as I read through it, I called her to tell her so. A man answered the phone, and for some reason I felt a stab of jealousy. Lilly came on quickly and said, "Joe! Do you like it?"

"It's great, Lilly. Just what I wanted. You are a very good writer, and I think I owe you another dinner. How about tonight?"

"Oh, I'd like to, Joe, but I already have other plans. I'm glad you like the piece, though. Why don't you call me later in the week?"

Sounded like the old brush off to me, and I had a hunch the other plans had answered the phone. Ah, well. I liked Lilly, and I would like to see more of her, but I had to face it: I'd just been dumped, but since that had happened before, it was no new experience. "Sure, Lilly. I'll call you sometime," I replied, and put the phone down.

I had no sooner put the phone down than it rang. "Hello?"

"Mr. Garth?"

"Yes."

"Mr. Garth, I read about you in the paper this morning, and I really need your help. I've lost my house, and if I don't get some money from somewhere, my family and I will be on the streets. Could you see your way clear to loaning me $20,000.00? I'd pay it back as soon as I can."

I was stunned by the call. How could some perfect stranger call me and boldly ask for twenty thousand dollars? "Look, mister, I'm real sorry that you're in trouble, but I don't know who you are. You might be sitting in a mansion calling me. Tell me some more about yourself, and I'll meet with you somewhere. I won't give you $20,000.00, but I could rent you a motel room for a week or so until you get on your fe..." The phone went dead before I could even finish the word. Now, what was that all about?

Unfortunately I was about to find out that the newspaper feature I was so proud of would bring me nothing but trouble. My phone rang almost non-stop the rest of the afternoon. At first, I answered it and tried to be polite, but finally I just left it off the hook to get some peace.

When I went down to help Tom feed – it was Roy's day off – I was still amazed at the calls. "Tom," I said, "that feature article about me came out in the paper today, and I've had phone calls from strangers all afternoon asking me for money. Can you believe that?"

Tom shook his head. "I reckon there are a lot of folks who think because you've got money you should give them some. I wonder how they'd feel if the boot was on the other foot?" He paused and looked down, kind of shy. "Joe, I sure want to thank you for hiring me here. You know I liked working for the Slash T, but I didn't get to do much cowboy work there. Anyway, thanks. This job's better than a whole lot of money to me."

I smiled at the young man. "Well, Tom, you're going to earn whatever you get here, and I'd say you've made a good start. Get Roy to show you some of his rope tricks. Don't tell him I said so, but he's pretty good."

We did the chores in peace, and I went back to the house.

The first thing Monday morning I called Miles Moore. I didn't know much about telephone technology, but I figured a real estate broker would, so I told Miles about the phone calls, and asked him how I could listen to the calls I wanted to and still have some privacy. "Joe, the phone company can give you a new unlisted number, and they can leave the other number active as voice mail only. Then, you can screen the calls before deleting them. Once you have your new number, only give it to people you want to have it. Do you have a cell phone?"

"No, but I was thinking about getting one."

"Do it, and guard that number carefully. That gives you another secure line to call out on."

"Thanks, Miles. Maybe if I just ignore the calls those people will give up and go away."

"Don't count on it, Joe. There are a lot of people in this world who make a living out of getting money from other people. And be careful about any deals that sound too good to be true: they usually are."

I spent the rest of the morning in the office getting the phone situation settled, figuring that as long as I was using the line, no one could call in. Sitting there looking out the window with a phone to my ear made me realize how I hated being inside so much, and I thought that maybe I needed a secretary to do office work for me. Maybe I'd ask Lilly about that…or maybe not.

Rita was in the house cleaning and singing, and she really brightened up the place. The phone was still ringing between times I was using it, and once or twice I had Rita answer in Spanish, but most of the time I answered it myself and said, "Sorry, but you've got the wrong guy."

Then, just as I was about to go out to the barns, the phone rang again, and I answered it with resignation. "Is that Mr. Garth?" the caller asked.

"Who wants to know?" I replied.

There was a chuckle at the other end. "I'll bet your phone's been ringing off the hook, hasn't it?"

"Yep. Now, what's your name and how much do you want?" I tried to always be a nice guy, and I didn't like to be rude to people, but my patience was wearing thin.

"Mr. Garth, my name is Ralph Richardson. I've got a place down by Jacksboro, and I've got an option on a ranch that adjoins me on the west that is going up for an estate sale. It's the old Bar M, and it covers about 20 sections in Jack and Young counties. I'd like to talk to you about investing in the place."

Well, now, I was interested in this request. Many of the calls I'd received had been from people wanting me to invest in projects, from automatic potato peelers, to self-mulching porta-potties, but this was the first one that made sense. "Well,

Mr. Richardson, if you want to come over here and talk about it, I've got some time this afternoon. How about 2:00 p.m.?"

Richardson quickly agreed, and I gave him directions, and then I told Rita the man's name and asked her to be sure and let him in.

The phone was ringing again as I left the house, and I heard Rita say, "Quien es?"

CHAPTER TEN

Ralph Richardson arrived a bit early, and Rita ushered him into the den where Roy and I were discussing rotating cattle pastures. Introductions were made, though I didn't mention why Richardson was there. Roy left to go back down to the barns, and I invited my guest to sit down.

"Now, then, Mr. Richardson. Tell me what you have in mind."

I looked the man over as he began to speak. He was dressed much as I was in clean range clothes and brushed up boots. Richardson looked to be in his fifties, and his hands were rough and work scarred. His face had the weathered look of an outdoor man, his hair was graying, and his words were pure cow country.

He told me how he had come to have an option on the property. "I was interested in the Bar M before old Carl died, so he gave me the option. He was not well at the time, so I made sure the option contract was solid enough to stand after his death. However, it runs out the first of the year, which gives me 18 days to come up with the money. The 1st National Bank of Jacksboro will give me a mortgage, but I've got to come up with a 20% down payment.

"The option is for $300.00 an acre, and that times 12,800 acres comes to three million eight hundred and forty thousand. That means I've got to come up with $768,000.00 by December 31, or I can't exercise the option." He paused for a minute. None of the figures Richardson quoted were written down, so he had obviously worked these things out long before.

"How much do you have, Mr. Richardson?"

"Well, I've been lucky enough to have a few producing oil wells drilled on my place, and I've saved my money. My wife died several years ago, and my only child, a daughter, is out of college and has a job right here in Wichita Falls, so I don't have a lot of expenses. I've managed to gather up $310,000.00, so I need an extra $458,000.00 for the down payment."

I was interested, but I was also cautious, and I remembered Miles admonition, "If it looks too good to be true, it probably is."

"If I furnish the $458,000.00, what do I get for my money?" Joe asked

"Well, I figure the payments on the loan will be pretty

well taken care of by oil royalties. Then there's a nice herd of cattle on the place, black baldy cows with Black Angus bulls, that can be bought, and I thought I'd go ahead and try to lump them in with the deal, so there'd be income from the cows, too. You could have interest on your money, or a working partnership, or any other arrangement that I can afford."

"I don't really need a working partnership, Mr. Richardson, since I've already got this place to take care of, and interest sounds nice, but I think I've got a better idea. I'll give you the $458,000.00, and I'll be a silent partner in the business. I'll take a fifteen percent share in the place. You put my income back into cows and I'll let you know if I need anything. From time to time you can let me know how things are going."

Richardson's face was suddenly all smiles. "You mean it?" he said. "Just like *that* you're going in with me?"

I laughed at his expression. "You know, Ralph, I've had a lot of crazy people call me with all kinds of schemes they want me to invest in, but I didn't know anything about their ideas. Now you come along with a deal that I can understand because I do know about cattle and ranch land, and I understand the risks involved. The cow market goes up and down, and usually when you've got the best critters, the prices are the lowest, but I know all of that. If I'm going to invest money, I'd just as soon it was with someone like you.

"Now, did you bring the paperwork and maps of the place?"

"You bet I did, Joe. Just let me run out to the pickup and get 'em."

We spent the rest of the afternoon going over the paperwork, and I asked Ralph to stay and eat with me. At the end of the evening I gave him a check for $458,000.00, almost too many numbers to go on the small piece of paper, and I told him that if he had any problems depositing it in the bank to give me a call. We shook hands on the deal, and Ralph went away a happy man.

The next day, Monday, it was not Ralph Richardson or his

banker that called, it was Mr. Argus from First American Commerce. "Mr. Garth," Argus said in a breezy friendly voice with a phony ring to it, "I just heard from Sam Blum over at 1st National in Jacksboro. That was a sizeable check you gave that rancher. If you want to rethink, I can tell Blum not to honor it. That ranch option may not be the best investment you can make, and if you let Richardson talk you into investing money when you really didn't want to, I can take care of things for you."

I was silent for a bit as anger began to build in me. Normally, it took a lot to make me mad, and I rarely got angry at anything, but Argus was pushing his luck. "Mr. Argus," I said in a tight voice, "you are my banker, not my employer. When you see a large check come through with my signature on it, you should call to see if I really wrote it or not. That's good business. But you do not tell me who to write checks to, or how much they should be for. Now, you have a choice here. You can tell your friend in Jacksboro to honor that check immediately, or I will personally come to *your* bank and cash out my account. Do you understand me?" I had not raised my voice, but my anger must have traveled down the phone wire.

"I'm sorry, Mr. Garth, and you're right. It is not up to me to advise you unless you ask for it. I was just trying to help."

"No, sir, you were not. You were trying to mind my business rather than your own. Now, what do you intend to do?"

He answered in a subdued voice. "I will call Sam Blum right now and tell him to cash the check, and I'll not try to tell you what to do. I assure you that nothing like this will ever happen again."

"In other words, Argus, you don't want to lose my account. Fine, just so we understand each other. Do as you say, and I'll put you on probation," and I hung up the phone.

Still angry, not a feeling I liked, I went down the barn and saddled Buck. A long ride would cool me off and put things back into perspective.

CHAPTER ELEVEN

Christmas was looming, and I wondered what to do about it, though the day had not meant much to me since my folks died. I didn't have any family living close by, but I did have a sister in San Francisco. She called and asked if I'd like to come there for the holidays, but I turned her down. We'd never been close, and I didn't like the city by the bay all that much.

This year Christmas would be on Thursday, so I told the hands to take off on Wednesday and not come back until Monday. I would do the feeding while they were gone. I gave Rita the same amount of time off, and she invited me to have Christmas dinner with her family, but I thanked her and said I had other plans.

At the Slash T I'd always volunteered to stay and feed the stock while the cowboys and ranch hands with families went home for Christmas. My *other plans* for this Christmas day consisted of a bologna sandwich and a day spent napping in front of the TV.

By mid-afternoon I was bored silly, so I went out to saddle Buck and ride over the pastures. It was a nice day, not real warm, but not cold either, and Buck and I both enjoyed the ride. I left the pasture up by the road for last, and I was just coming near the front gate when I noticed a red sports car parked along the bar ditch.

At first I thought it might be a reporter, though Christmas day seemed an odd time for a newsy to be around, but as I drew closer, I saw that the car had a flat tire, and a very pretty girl with long dark hair was trying to change it. She was concentrating on the tire, and she didn't hear Buck's soft hoof steps.

I dismounted at the gate and punched the numbers in the pad to open it. The girl heard the whine of the opener, and turned to look. "Could you use a hand, ma'am?" I asked.

"I sure could, cowboy," she replied with a stunning smile.

I led Buck through the gate and ground hitched him near the road. "My name's Joe Garth," I said with a smile.

She held her hand out to shake, "I'm Tommie Manning," she said.

"Well, Ms Manning, let's see if we can get your tire changed." I quickly positioned the jack, loosened the wheel nuts, jacked up the car and removed the tire, and then reached into the trunk to pull out the ridiculous donut spare. "You won't want to go too far on that tire, Ms Manning. It's meant to only take you to a place where you can get the other one fixed."

"Oh, I've only got a few miles to go, Mr. Garth. My parents live on down this road. In fact, I think their property shares a fence with yours. They told me they had a new neighbor."

"Do you know anything about me, Ms Manning?"

"Why, no, should I? And please all me Tommie."

"Not at all, and I'm Joe. Why don't you drive slowly and I'll follow along on Buck just to make sure you get there." She gave me a smile, climbed into her car and moved off down the road. I swung into Buck's saddle and followed the little red car, riding in the grass-covered bar ditch.

When we reached my southern fence line, I could see ranch buildings in the distance. Tommie pulled into the gravel-covered driveway that led to the buildings, and stopped the car. As I rode up and swung down, she got out and said, "Thanks for following along, Joe. Since it's Christmas day, if you don't have any other plans, why don't you come over for Christmas dinner? We'll eat at six o'clock because my mom can't do much in the kitchen, and I usually cook when I'm here. There'll just be the four of us, if you come."

"Why, thank you, Tommie. I am pretty tired of my own company, so if you think it will be all right with your folks, I'll go put Buck up and do the chores and come back at 6:00."

"Oh, my folks will think it's fine, but I better warn you, my mom's a terrible match-maker, and she thinks I need a husband, so you'll have to be careful."

I laughed. "I'll take the risk," I said, and when I turned Buck to go back along the road I continued to myself, "and that's not a bad prospect."

"What did you say?" Tommie asked.

I pulled up. "Oh, I just said having a home cooked meal is not a bad prospect. I was going to have a bologna sandwich for supper." Tommie waved and got into her car, and I went back along the road. "That girl's got great ears, Buck. And the rest of her's not bad, either."

When I got back to the ranch, I put Buck up and fed him and the rest of the animals. The sky to the north had taken on a dark brooding look, and I figured another cold spell with maybe some snow or ice was coming in, a serious blue norther. I made sure all gates were closed, and went back to the house to change clothes.

Tommie's parents were as friendly and welcoming as ranchers everywhere. They were in their mid-sixties, and I could see why Mrs. Manning didn't do much cooking. She was seated in a wheelchair, and she didn't shake hands because hers were gnarled with what looked like bad arthritis. She said, "Why, you're the young man who won the lottery, aren't you Mr. Garth?"

I looked sheepish, and I caught just a hint of a gleam of surprise in Tommie's eye. "Yes, ma'am, I reckon I am."

"Oh, forgive me for that thoughtless comment, Joe," Mrs. Manning said when she saw the look on my face. "We're very happy to have you spend Christmas with us."

Fred Manning, Tommie's father, called me into the den to sit by a roaring fire while the women finished the dinner preparations.

"Sorry we haven't been over to welcome you to the area, Joe. Lillian and I don't get out much anymore."

"No problem, Mr. Manning, I understand. By the way, I sure saw some good lookin' horses in that pen south of your barn. Seems like we share a liking for good horseflesh."

We were deep into a discussion about horses when Tommie called us to come to the dining room to see if the tantalizing smells that filled the house lived up to their promise. A small roasted turkey was situated in the middle of the table, with dishes of mashed potatoes and gravy, corn and green beans, sausage dressing and black-eyed peas, along with a large platter of homemade rolls.

I remembered my manners and held Tommie's chair for her, and then sat down across the table. We all bowed our heads while Fred asked the Lord to bless the food, and then began to eat.

When I felt like I couldn't eat another bite, Tommie brought a pot of coffee and a pecan pie to the table and sat the pie in front of me. Not wanting to give offense, I manfully cut out a large piece. "I don't really know where I'm going to put this," I said, "but it looks so good I know I won't have to chew. It'll just naturally melt in my mouth." I aimed my compliment at Tommie, but it missed its mark.

The other three laughed at me, and Lillian Manning said, "Why thank you, Joe. One thing I can still do is bake pies, and since Fred's favorite is pecan, he doesn't even mind cracking the nuts for me." I joined in the laughter at that comment.

I couldn't keep from comparing my large cold house with the Manning's small warm one. Rita had hung some Christmas decorations around at home, but I'd told her not to do too much as there wouldn't be anybody in for Christmas anyway.

In the Manning's den there was a large Christmas tree with brightly wrapped gifts piled underneath. The mantel was decorated with holly and a long wreath, a wide ribbon with cards pinned to it hung in the doorway, while candles burned in several colorful holders.

I helped Tommie clear the table and put the dishes in the washer, enjoying bumping into her from time to time in the small kitchen. When the dishwasher was humming away, we joined Lillian and Fred in the den. "Joe, I noticed some fine looking Angus cattle in the breaks near our fence line. Are they registered?" Fred asked.

"They sure are, Fred. I figure blooded cattle don't eat any more than stockers, and I've always like Black Angus, so when my ship came in I found that little herd at a dispersal sale and bought 'em."

The talk went on about horses and cattle, with Lillian and Tommie joining in. Lillian had been a ranch girl when Fred married her, and she knew all there was to know about cattle and horses. And, of course, Tommie was raised on her folk's ranch, so nothing we discussed went over her head.

I learned that Tommie had graduated from the University of Oklahoma and now worked for a marketing firm in Oklahoma City, though she came back home as often as she could. Lillian put in that her daughter was still single without even a steady boyfriend. Fred and I shouted with laughter, and Tommie blushed. "Mom! That's not fair. Just because it's Christmas you can't go around telling people about my love life."

"That's just the problem, Tommie Manning," Lillian said. "You don't *have* a love life. Why, when I was twenty-seven Fred and I had been married for eight years, and you were five-years-old."

Tommie managed to move the conversation in another direction, and the evening passed with a lot of laughter and friendship.

Finally, I got to his feet and said, "Well, folks, it's about time for me to head off." I went to Mrs. Manning and touched the back of her hand. "Ma'am, I don't know when I've had a better time. My mama always said a warm home is the reflection of the lady who lives there, and truer words were never spoken. And I can sure see where your daughter gets her beauty," I turned and looked at Fred, "and it's not from her daddy!"

They all laughed, and Lillian actually blushed a bit. "Oh, you smooth talkin' cowboy. You sound just like Fred when he was sparking me. But thank you, Joe. We hope to see you over here real often."

Fred added his invitation as he shook my hand. "Come over and see my horses one day, Joe."

"I'd like that, Fred. After the first of the year I'm going to buy a good stud and some mares. I'll sure want you to take a look at them, too."

Tommie put on a coat and went out with me to the pickup. "Why, Joe Garth," she said. "I'm surprised you don't have a big new truck with all the bells and whistles, what with you winning the lottery and all."

I grinned. "I know, and I'm going to get one some day, but

for now, Old Green gets me around okay."

"Why didn't you want me to know you had won a bunch of money, Joe?"

"I didn't mean to offend you, Tommie. It's just that I've grown kind of leery of folks makin' up to me because of the money, and I wanted you to like plain old Joe Garth, not the man who won the lottery."

She gave me a teasing grin, batted her eyes, and said in mock honeyed tones, "Why Mr. Garth! Why ever would you think that of little ole me?"

We laughed together, and I didn't think I'd ever heard a laugh that I liked so much. I told her how much I liked her parents and their home, and Tommie thanked me for making her mother feel special. I opened the pickup door and stood leaning on it. "Well," I said, "goodnight, Tommie Manning."

"Good night, Joe Garth," Tommie replied. And she quickly stood on tiptoe, brushed my lips with hers, and then whirled and ran back to the house calling out, "Merry Christmas, Joe!"

"Merry Christmas!" I called back.

And it was a Merry Christmas, after all.

CHAPTER TWELVE

By mid-January when the horse sale took place, Tommie and I were seeing a lot of each other. Tommie was coming to her folk's place most weekends, and since the sale was on a Saturday, I asked her if she wanted to go along. "I'd love to, Joe. I like to see good horses."

The sale was at the legendary King Ranch just outside Kingsville, Texas. We took a very early flight from the Wichita Falls Regional Airport to Love Field in Dallas, and then on Southwest Airlines to Corpus Christi International. We arrived in mid-morning, rented a car and drove the fifty miles to Kingsville, passing through the gate by showing my invitation card, and driving the short way up a winding drive past the magnificent white house Captain King had built for his bride. The road led on out onto the coastal plain where the horse barns were located.

The sale was to start at one o'clock, and a special pit barbeque beef meal was laid on beginning at 11:30. Pit barbequed beef was nothing like the weak stuff served at roadside BBQ stands. A day before the auction, a whole side of beef that had been marinated in a special sauce, wrapped in burlap and placed on a grate over a glowing bed of coals in a deep pit, nearly grave-sized, dug just for the occasion. Once the meat was in position, a cover of tin was laid on top, and then dirt was shoveled into the pit until it was completely filled. The beef slow cooked for twenty-four hours, and soon it would be dug up and served piping hot along with red beans and cornbread. Nothing could compare with the taste of real pit-barbequed beef.

I wanted to look at the horses up for sale before the auction began, so Tommie and I went to the barns and watched as the stable hands took the horses from their boxes and walked them up and down in front of closed-faced potential buyers. I'd read up on one stallion in particular that I was interested in. The deep sorrel quarter horse with the white blaze down his face could trace his bloodlines back to the original Old Sorrel, the King Ranch's famous herd sire. When this horse, Handy's Own, was led out, I could see that he was everything he was cracked up to be, and he would be very expensive. Like the other men and women who were there to buy, I carefully kept my face straight as we watched the horse move.

To show how gentle he was, a young boy, certainly no

older than ten, was given a leg up onto the broad sorrel back, and he rode the horse around without saddle or bridle.

Tommie had been watching my face, and those of the other watchers. She said in a low voice, "Is that the one you want?"

I slowly turned my head and looked at her, smiling just a bit and winking, but I didn't answer.

"Oops," she said, putting her hand over her mouth. "I wasn't supposed to ask that, was I?"

I tucked her arm under mine and turned to slowly walk away. When we were quite a ways off, I said. "That's the horse, but he'll go high. All of those other folks there looking on with no expression will be bidding on him too, so if I want him, I'll have to pay the price."

The clanging of an iron rod on a chuck wagon triangle announced that the beef had been dug up, and it was time to eat. The food was every bit as good as expected, and Tommie said she wouldn't mind going to more horse sales if they all fed like the King Ranch.

At 1:00 p.m. exactly, the bidding started. I intended to bid on some good mares as well as the stallion, and I bought four for a total of $105,000.00 during the next two hours. At three o'clock, the auctioneer took a break and the stallions were led out. The first one, an untried two-year-old, went for eighty thousand dollars, and next, a proven four-year-old topped out at $120,000.00. Then a hush fell on the crowd as Handy's Own was led out to the ring. His coat glistened in the sunshine, and he was as calm as a gelding. The auctioneer started his spiel by reciting the horse's bloodlines, and then he began to talk about his get. Handy's Own was six years old, and his progeny had won an astounding list of cutting horse futurities, roping competitions, and horse shows.

The auctioneer started the bidding at $100,000.00, and that figure was quickly run up to $200,000.00. There the bidding slowed. I had not entered a bid yet, and Tommie was looking a question at me, but I ignored her. I had spotted the two major bidders, and I watched as one of them raised her card to up the bid to $225,000.00. The auctioneer went on and one of the other bidders nodded for another $25,000.00.

With the bid at $250,000.00, the auctioneer was really working, but the woman did not raise the man's bid, and the auctioneer went on. Finally, he paused in his litany, and then said, "Are we all through?" He looked at the woman who shook her head, and then started to say, "Going once. Going..." and I raised my card, and said, "And twenty-five."

The man who had made the last bid was ahead of me, and he couldn't see who had raised him, he turned and looked, but I avoided his eye. The auctioneer said, "We have a new bidder," and he turned back to the man I was challenging. "It's up to you, sir."

The man waited for a hundred heartbeats, and then slowly shook his head. "All done then?" the auctioneer asked as his eyes swept the crowd. "All right, going once, going twice, going the third time, and sold to the gentleman holding card number 32 for $275,000.00."

Tommie hugged my arm. "You bought him!" she cried.

I grinned down at her. "I sure did," I replied.

Once the check was given and I had made arrangements for the five horses, four mares and Handy's Own, to be shipped, Tommie and I left the King ranch and traveled back to the Corpus airport. It was late when the American Eagle landed at Wichita Falls, and later still when I stopped my pickup in the Manning's driveway. Both of us were tired, and our goodnights were over quickly. Tommie said she'd come over in the morning and cook my breakfast, and after a hasty hug and kiss she ran into the house.

I rolled into bed with a sigh. I had my ranch, my horses and cattle and a good-looking woman to date, what more could a man ask?

CHAPTER THIRTEEN

It was a cold Monday morning, and I'd had just come in from showing Roy how I wanted the horses stabled to find the phone ringing. Rita answered and told me my accountant was on the line. That was odd. It was only a few minutes after 8:00, and Josh rarely started work before nine. "What's up, Josh?"

"Joe, I'm starting to work on your tax return today, and

I think we should have a conference. Any chance you can come see me today or tomorrow?"

"Well, it will have to be today, Josh. I bought some horses Saturday down at the King Ranch, and they're supposed to be delivered tomorrow so I want to hang around here. How about this morning some time?"

"Sure. Would 9:00 suit you? I'll shift some things around."

"Fine, Josh. I'll be there."

I had my breakfast and headed out to the garage to the new Ford pickup. As a late Christmas present to myself I'd gone to the Ford dealership in Wichita Falls and bought a deep green F250 extended cab pickup with all the bells and whistles as Tommie had suggested. I opened the garage door and backed out, closing the door behind me. In twenty minutes I was seated across from Josh Williamson, my CPA.

"Okay, Josh, enough mystery. Why did I have to come in to see you?"

"Joe, I've been going over your accounts and I don't know if you're aware of how much money you've spent since you won the lottery."

"Well, I've got a rough idea, but I haven't kept track of it all. That's why I hired the bookkeeper you suggested. She sends me a statement each month, but I'll admit I don't go over it very carefully. So how much have I spent?"

"You started with $4,110,396.42 in October. You paid $100,000.00 down on the ranch, and you made two mortgage payments of $6123.80 for a total of $12,247.60. $84,975.00 went for farm equipment, and $89,000.00 for cattle. Salaries and benefits for two months amounted to $6,641.87. Then you invested $458,000.00 in the Jacksboro ranch. All of that's a total of $750,804.47. That means that you have spent over 18% of the original amount. Are you aware that you've spent so much?"

"Well, I didn't know to the penny, but I had a pretty good idea. So, what's the problem, Josh?"

Josh looked at me with amazement. "What's the problem, Joe? If you continue to spend the way you have, in six years you'll be broke!"

A small light began to come on in my mind. It was Argus at the bank that had recommended this CPA. Before answering, I took a thin wallet out of my shirt pocket, opened it up, and laid it down on the accountant's desk. "That's my driver's license, Josh. If you'll look at the birth date you'll find that I am well over twenty-one. In fact, I'll never see thirty again, and I've got forty pretty well cornered. In other words, Josh, I don't need a nanny.

"Now, I have a question for you. Have you been talking about my business to Argus at First American Commerce?"

The look on Josh's face told me he was guilty. "Look, Joe, we're just trying to help you," he said weakly.

"Uh-huh. Did I ask you to help me?" I asked as I returned the wallet to my shirt pocket.

"No, but an accountant always tries to have his client's best interest at heart. I felt it was my duty to call this matter to your attention."

"Josh, I believe you have a partner in this business, don't you?"

"Yes, Harold Duckworth is my partner."

"Is he the senior partner, or are you?"

"Well, he is. Why do you ask?"

"Josh, if you were a cowhand working for me and you tried to tell me how to run the ranch, I'd fire you in a heartbeat. Now, if as an employee you made a suggestion for a change that would save the ranch money, or make more profit, I'd listen. Your problem, and that of Argus at the bank, is that you assume because I've made my living for most of my life on the back of a horse, I don't have any common sense. You might be right, but you *have* no right to assume anything about me, because you are my employee.

"You have not suggested to me how I can make the money I have grow, or how the things I've bought can be more profitable. You've only taken it upon yourself to tell this dumb cowboy that he's throwing his money around. Well, Josh, as my employee, you've failed the test. You're fired. As of right now you are no longer my accountant." I had been raised to respect other people's privacy, particularly about business. I certainly did that myself, and I expected the same courtesy in return. Furthermore, I did not treat people with contempt, and I didn't appreciate it when others, particularly my banker and my accountant, two men who made money from my money, treated me with a superior attitude.

I stood to my feet and towered over a very worried CPA. "Now, if you want to keep my account in the business, you have Mr. Duckworth call me this morning."

As I closed the door I looked back at the shocked face of Josh Williamson, and winked at him.

I was in the horse barn with Tom and Roy when the call came from Harold Duckworth. "Mr. Garth," he began, "first I want to apologize for my junior partner's poor behavior, and then I want to say that if you're not confident that we can work for you in a professional way, I will personally recommend several other accounting firms that you might want to check out. I am embarrassed and ashamed that you were treated in such a shabby manner."

"Mr. Duckworth, I'm kind of busy right now, but I'll think about this and call you this afternoon."

"Fine, sir, fine. Just call anytime. My receptionist will have orders to put you through to me immediately, and if I'm out, she will forward your call to my cell phone."

That was more like it. I was going to spend more money; that's what it was for, wasn't it? And I didn't want to have anyone, an accountant or a banker or anyone else, pulling me up short. Anyway, most of the things I bought would make money in the long run. I knew what I was doing, didn't I? Later in the afternoon, I called Duckworth and asked him to personally take over my account. I also told him about my recent purchases, and the CPA replied, "Fine, Mr. Garth, I'll be in touch from time to time to let you know how things are progressing."

Tuesday morning brought a call that the horse trailers were in Fort Worth and the drivers needed final instructions on how to get to the ranch. I gave them gladly and let Roy know over the intercom that the horses would arrive later in the morning.

When the two low-body horse vans with the Running W King Ranch brand pulled up outside the horse barn, everyone – including Rita – came out to see the horses unloaded. The stallion came out of his trailer first. He had been transported alone as befitted his status, and as he calmly walked down the low ramp I caught my breath at the beauty of the animal. Handy's Own, to be nicknamed "Handy," was led to his large box stall at the east end of the alleyway and closed in after I inspected him thoroughly. I wondered how my friend Handy at the Slash T would like having a quarter horse stallion with the same name. Probably he'd brag about it and claim kinship.

While I was looking at the stud, the men were unloading the four mares and leading them to their own large boxes. Each box had a gated opening to single long runs, and a further opening to a large pipe-fenced paddock. I went to each of the mares, inspecting them as carefully as I had the stallion. All four were in perfect shape.

I signed the release papers the head driver handed me, and the trucks pulled away.

Buck and the other geldings pastured on the south side of the horse barn were sounding now. They smelled the stallion and the new mares, and they would like to have a closer look, but that wasn't in the cards. Roy, Tom and I went into the barn to take care of feed and water, and Rita and Jose went back to their kitchens.

"Joe, I don't think I've ever seen better horseflesh in my life," Roy said as they looked at the stud over the stall door.

"Someday, Roy, I'll take you and Tom down to the King Ranch. They've got pastures full of the finest quarter horse mares in the world. And the studs they have are all world class just like this fella."

Two weeks later I invited Tommie and her parents to come for Sunday dinner, and to see the new horses. Of course, Tommie had already seen them, but this would be the first viewing by Lillian and Fred.

Normally, Rita had Sunday off, but she volunteered to come in on the morning the Mannings were invited and have a meal ready before she left for church. I was very pleased with her, as I'd intended to have the meal catered, so I told her there would be a bonus in her paycheck for the month. "Oh, Mr. Garth, that's not necessary. You already pay me far more than any housekeeper I know. And besides, you give me time off whenever I ask for it. No, you keep the bonus, and I'll make the meal."

I smiled at her and decided to give her the bonus anyway.

By 10:00 the meal was ready, and Rita gave me my instructions. "The tamales are fine in the warming oven, and the flour tortillas are here. Just put them in the microwave and warm them up for two minutes. The rest of the meal is in the big oven, and all you have to do is pull the dishes out, put them on the table, and then turn the oven off. There's tea in the pitcher in the refrigerator, and coffee ready to be made. For dessert, I made big sopapillas because you like them so much. When you take the tortillas out of the microwave, put the sopapillas in, and just before you are ready for them, turn on the microwave for one minute. Okay?"

I'd been writing down the instructions. "I think I can do that, Rita. Maybe the Mannings will think I cooked this all myself."

Rita laughed loudly. "I think Miss Tommie knows you too well to believe you can cook." I laughed with her and saw her to the door where her son was waiting to take her to church.

The Mannings arrived just at noon, and I went out to help Fred wheel Lillian's chair through the wide double doors and into the dining room. Once we were all seated with steaming platters of Rita's finest loading the table down, I looked at Fred and asked him to bless the food as he had done on Christmas day.

There was not much talk at first as all of us scooped the delicious Mexican food onto our plates and began to dig in. When I came up for air, I said, "Rita, the lady who makes my house run, fixed all of this food this morning. I told her I thought I would try to pass it off as my own cooking, but she said I'd never fool Tommie, so I guess I won't try that one."

Fred chuckled and confided that *he* had become a pretty good cook in the last few years, and Lillian laughed at that. "Oh, yes, dear, you're a great cook, if a person likes eggs, sausage, bacon and hash browns."

"Well," I said, "I may not be much of a cook, and I can't tease your stomachs, but I think I do have something to show you after we eat that will fill your *eyes*. We'll go out and take a look at the new horses."

When the dishes were cleared away and Tommie had a new pot of coffee brewing, we all put on our coats and went out the back door. The builders had added a winding blacktopped walk that sloped from the deck down to the horse barns, and it was no problem to wheel Lillian down the smooth surface. We came first to the large paddock on the south side of the barn where the mares were held. Roy and I had been breeding the mares as they came into season, and we hoped to soon have them all safely in foal to Handy's Own.

When the Mannings had their fill of looking at the quiet mares, I wheeled Lillian down the center aisle of the barn to the east end where the stallion was kept. He had a spacious box stall that opened on the southeast to a large grassy paddock. When he saw me, Handy nickered, came to the fence and stuck his head over. He and I had developed a special horse/man relationship since he'd been on the ranch. I talked to him, and opened the gate to let him out into the alleyway without a halter or a lead rope.

Handy immediately went to Lillian and dropped his soft nose into her cupped hands. He whiffled at her hands, and then looked right into her eyes. Tommie's mother laughed with pleasure. "Joe," Fred said, "looks to me like you've just lost a horse."

I grinned at the sight. "Well, now, Fred, I like to think I'm a pretty good judge of horseflesh, and it looks like you're a pretty good judge of women. Handy seems to know who the head of your household is."

"He sure got that right," Fred said.

Tommie came over to me, stood on tiptoes and kissed me on the cheek. She didn't say anything, but her eyes were bright and they thanked me for once again making her mother feel special.

After looking at the horses, we all went back to the house and had coffee, and at 3:30 Fred and Lillian went out to their car to travel the short distance back home. Tommie and I watched as they drove up the winding drive, and then went back into the house. The temperature was dropping and it kind of looked like another norther was on the way, but I built up the fire in the huge stone fireplace, and we sat close together on the small loveseat in front of it.

"You know, Joe, you've got quite a way with women. You really made Mom feel good today."

"And how about you, Tommie Manning? Did I make you feel good?"

She snuggled closer and smiled. "You *always* make me feel good, Mr. Garth. My friends at work laugh at me because I make so many excuses to leave work early on Fridays. I can't seem to wait to see you. Why is that do you suppose?"

I was smiling now, too. "Why, I guess it's because spring is coming," he replied. "You know, spring is just made for romance, and you're a real romantic."

She gently nudged me in the ribs with her elbow. "And I suppose you're *not* a romantic, Joe Garth? You with your ideal ranch, and your cattle and horses? That's not romantic? And how about taking me to a horse sale at the King Ranch, of all places. Now, some girls might think that was too crude for romance, but not me. I think you knew all along that would bring out the romance in me."

We were kissing when the back door opened and Rita's voice floated through, "I'm back, Mr. Garth. Do you want some supper?" When there was no answer, Rita came into the kitchen, and out of the corner of my eye I saw her look around the corner into the den. Seeing our heads close together, she smiled, and I heard her whisper, "Ah, amor," and tiptoe away.

CHAPTER FOURTEEN

The weeks slid by, and I forgot all about CPAs and bankers as I helped the men with calving. The registered Black Angus cows began dropping their calves in mid-march, and I wanted to see them all. Though over the years I'd watched many calves born, even helped some of them into the world when a cow was having a problem, the miracle of birth still amazed me.

For most people who worked with cattle everyday, spring calving was a time of hard work and happiness. I was no exception, but this year was different. I still had that good feeling, but with an extra lift; now when I saw a new calf emerge, I also experienced a sense of great satisfaction, for all the calves came from my own cows.

On the big ranches, first-calf heifers were usually separated into a small pasture close to the ranch buildings so they could be watched carefully as the time for delivery drew near, while the older cows dropped their calves out in the big pastures. But on a small place like the Rafter JG, all of the cows were held in a small pasture close to the barn where they could easily be checked several times a day. We even had a birthing pen that a cow could be moved to if there might be trouble.

At Roy's suggestion, I hired another cowboy to help with the work, and soon there were healthy little black calves running and kicking all over the place. Luke Lewis, the new man, came from the Panhandle, and he jumped right in with both feet, showing what a top hand he was.

It was Friday, a lovely March morning, when I went down to the cow barn to see if there were any new arrivals. The sun was just coming up, and I could hear the mockingbird in the huge live oak near the bunkhouse tuning up. It was one of those mornings that made a man glad to be alive.

At the calving pen I watched along with Roy and Luke while a first-calf heifer labored to bring a fine bull calf into the world. We did not usually interfere with the birth process, for we wanted the cows to birth naturally, but we also wanted to be around to help in case there was a problem. The young cow heaved and the calf's nose appeared, laid gently on his front feet. Another heave, and the whole head appeared. Finally, with a grunt from the cow, out popped the baby, shrouded in pieces of the birth-sack.

The young cow was still lying on her side recovering when the newborn calf began to move, rolling up on his chest.

Now the cow turned over and heaved to her feet, turning so her nose touched the baby. She began to lick him and murmur to him, cleaning and stimulating her calf, at times almost rolling him over with her rough tongue.

The three of us watched from the fence until the baby struggled to his feet and wobbled to his mother's tight udder. When he had a teat pulled into his mouth and was sucking the first rich milk into his tiny belly, we turned to go with grins on our faces. "I'll be up at the house, Roy, if you need me," I said. No matter how many times I'd seen it, God's miracle of birth still filled me with wonder.

I made my way on up to the good smells of Rita's breakfast, and the happy sounds of her singing. Once again I thanked God for this wonderful woman.

I'd just finished my breakfast when the phone rang. Rita answered, and then brought the phone to me saying, "It's Lilly Walker."

"Hello, Lilly," I said. "How's everything in the newspaper business?"

"Hi, Joe. Everything's fine. I just hadn't heard from you in a while, so I thought I'd touch base. How's everything on the ranch?"

"Fine, Lilly. We've got new calves dropping all over the place, and it's good to be alive."

"New calves, huh? I'll bet they're cute." There was a request for an invitation buried in that sentence, but I ignored it.

"They are that. Of course, they're also money running around on four legs."

We exchanged a few more comments, ending our conversation pleasantly enough.

I sat in thought for a bit after hanging up. I'd really liked Lilly, but after a man, I assumed a boyfriend, answered the phone the last time I called, I had pretty well figured she was taken. Then, of course, there was Tommie. I'd picked up on the hint about coming out to see the new calves, but somehow I didn't think Tommie would be too happy about me inviting another pretty woman to the ranch.

The phone rang again as I was heading back out to the barns. I waited until Rita said with a mischievous smile that it was Tommie. "Joe," she cried in a breathless voice. "I'm stranded! My car has broken down in Chickasha. Can you help me?"

"Calm down, Tommie. Just tell me where you are, and I'll come get you."

"Oh, Joe, thanks. I didn't know what to do. I'm afraid my car is in bad shape. Anyway, take the first off ramp and come north of the toll way. Just after you pass the first stop light there's a garage on the left. The sign out front says Rowdy's Wrecker Service. They towed me in, and they said they'd work on my car, but I don't really like the looks of the place, or Rowdy himself. He's spending far more time looking at me than he is looking under the car hood. Twice he's tried to put his greasy hands on me. How fast can you get here?"

"It'll take me a couple of hours at least. Is there a fast food or a café nearby?"

"Well, about a block south of here there's what you call a 'little Scottish restaurant' on the east side of the street."

"Okay, now, listen, Tommie. Don't even look back, just walk away from the garage right now. Go to Mickey D's and sit there until I come. I know it will be a long wait, but you'll be safe there."

There was a pause. "But, Joe, I left my purse in the car. Shall I go back in and get it?"

"No. Just walk away. We'll get your purse when I get there."

"Okay, but please hurry."

"I'll call you when I'm on the road," I replied.

We disconnected and I went into the kitchen where Rita was working. After I told her where I was going, I said, "Rita, please tell Roy I'll be out of pocket for a while. I don't know when we'll be back, so don't hold lunch for me."

"Oh, Mr. Joe, I hope Miss Tommie's okay. I'll pray for you

both."

"Thanks, Rita. We'll probably need those prayers."

I was through Wichita Falls in record time, and before long I slowed down to cross the Red River. Usually an Oklahoma state policeman was stationed on the other side of the border at the top of the first long climb; sure enough he was there this time. I waved as I passed by. A few minutes later I entered the toll way, and ratcheted up my speed to just under eighty miles an hour. The speed limit was 75, but from past experience I'd learned that the cops wouldn't bother anyone doing less than eighty.

The miles flew by. Soon I was working my way through Lawton, past Fort Sill and back onto the toll way north of town. I'd been on the road just over two hours when I took the off ramp at Chickasha. I spotted Tommie immediately when I pulled into the parking lot at the fast food. When I jumped out of the pickup, she came running, throwing herself into my arms After a very nice kiss Tommie said, "I'm so glad to see you, Joe Garth. I mean, I'm always glad to see you, but I'm *really* glad this time."

I laughed at her. "Let's go get your car."

When we pulled into the driveway of the garage, I asked Tommie to stay in the pickup while I got out and walked into the large open door. Tommie's little red car sat in a bay with the hood up, but no one was around it. I looked it over and opened the driver's door, looking inside. I picked it up Tommie's purse lying on the seat and opened it. "Whatcha think you're doin', cowboy?"

I turned at the voice still holding the purse. "I'm checking my girlfriend's purse to make sure nothing's missing."

"You just put that purse back where you got it and get on outta here. She doesn't get her purse until she pays up." The man was big with long, lank hair hanging around his face. He wore grease stained blue coveralls, and a baseball cap stuck down on his head sideways. His face was pockmarked with what looked like chickenpox scars. The man was not only dirty, he was hog ugly.

I smiled at him, holding onto the purse. "Well, now. Why don't you just tell me what the bill is and I'll pay it."

"You're not payin' anything here, cowboy. I'm goin' to count to three, and you better be gone."

I really grinned at that one. This guy watched way too much TV. "Oh, I know why you're only going to count to three, Greasy. You can't count any higher, and you probably have to do that on your fingers. Go ahead, show me how much you know."

The big man gave a growl, pulled a long wrench out of his pocket, and launched himself at me, but he was slow. His first swipe with the wrench was almost laughable. I leaned back to let it miss and went under it. Using the man's momentum I just pushed him all the way around, grabbing the wrist of the hand holding the wrench as he swung by. Quick as wink I pushed Greasy's arm up high enough to get a yell of pain, bent him over and ran him head first into the concrete block wall. That was the end of the fight.

A yell brought me around to see two smaller versions of the big man coming through the office door. I didn't hesitate. Picking up the wrench the big man had dropped, I threw it at the two and charged right after it. Kicking one of them in the knee, I slugged the other one hard in the chest just over his heart. They both went down. "Stay down, both of you. If you try to get up, I'll come back and stomp you."

I looked in the office, but I didn't see anyone else. Coming back to the groggy man I'd run into the wall, I picked him up and hauled him into the office. "Did you repair the car, Greasy?"

"Yeah. It was just some loose plug wires. It runs."

"Okay, give me the bill, Greasy, and while you're doing that, keep in mind that I expect reasonable charges." I unplugged the phone cord from the jack and tossed it behind a parts-covered counter. Then I moved to the door and waved my arm at Tommie. When she stepped out of the truck, I called, "Come take a look and tell me if anything's missing."

Before Tommie could enter the office, the big man pulled open a top desk drawer and took Tommie's wallet out of it, tossing it at me. "Now, Greasy, that's the only smart thing I've seen you do today. Keep it up and you might just join the human race, oh, way down on the list, of course."

Tommie looked in her wallet. "The money's all here, but my Visa card is missing."

I looked at the mechanic without saying anything. He visibly wilted, and said, "Okay, cowboy. My boy's got it. The one huggin' his knee."

I went back out into the garage, and the "boy" pulled the credit card out of his pocket, wordlessly holding it up.

A search of the car revealed that nothing else was missing. Tommie got into the car and started it. It didn't run very well, but it did run. "Go on up to the parking lot where I met you and wait for me," I said with a grin. She looked pale and little frightened, but my grin reassured her.

When Tommie was gone, I went back into the office and looked at the bill Rowdy showed me. The tow was $60.00 and repairs were $20.00. I figured that was about half what he would have charged Tommie if I hadn't been there. I pulled a one hundred dollar bill out of my pocket to pay. Rowdy gave me back a twenty. "Now, Greasy, write me out a receipt. Make it out to Joe Garth and Tommie Manning, and sign your full name at the bottom." At the name Joe Garth, Rowdy gave a jerk looking at me with new eyes. He must have heard about the lottery.

Writing was not Rowdy's long suit, but he finally managed to get the receipt written and signed. I put it in my pocket. "Now, you greasy crook, if I ever hear that you've robbed or abused any other women, I'll come back and just naturally tear this place down around your ears. And if you try some scam with the cops, I'll also come back and take you to Sunday school. Do you understand me?"

The big man nodded his head, but hate filled his eyes.

I drove back to McDonalds and parked next to Tommie's car. She hugged me and said, "Thanks, cowboy. Now what?"

"Does your car run well enough to get you home?"

"I don't think so. It died twice on me just getting it here.

I'm afraid to take it out on the interstate."

"Okay, let's see if we can find another garage and get it fixed right."

After several phone calls, I drove the gasping red peril across the overpass to Anderson's garage, with Tommie following in the pickup. I was met by a middle-aged man in white coveralls with "Richard" stitched above the pocket. I told him about Tommie's experience with Rowdy, but not about the fight. The mechanic said he knew them by reputation, a bad reputation.

When Mr. Anderson hooked Tommie's car up to some electronic equipment, he said, "Well, it looks like your plugs are all shot. I don't know what's caused that, and it would take some time for me to figure it out. If you're not in a hurry, I'll get right on it."

"Problem is, we are in kind of a hurry," I said. "If you put new plugs in, do you think we could make it to Wichita Falls?"

"Yes, I think so. Do you have a garage you can take it to there?"

Tommie pulled a card out of her purse and showed it to Anderson. "This is where I have my car serviced. I'm sure if they can't do the work they can recommend someone for me."

We took cups of coffee from Mr. Anderson's pot and sat in the pickup while the man changed the spark plugs. Just an hour passed before he started the car. It ran smoothly, at least for now. Tommie paid the bill – $32.00 – got in and pulled onto the toll way with me following.

The trip back to Wichita Falls was uneventful. Once there, Tommie led me to Arnie's Quick Service, but he didn't do any mechanical work. However, he called the Nissan garage for us. They could take the car, so again I followed her.

It was late afternoon when everything was settled, so I suggested that Tommie call her parents so they wouldn't worry, and we'd stop somewhere for a bite to eat before going home. Over a lukewarm plate at a cafeteria, I said, "You know, Tommie, I think it's time for you to come back to Texas. Your folks aren't getting any younger, and they'd probably like to see more of you."

"Any other reason for wanting me to move back, Joe?"

"Well, yes, there is. I wouldn't want my wife living in Oklahoma. Long distance marriages never really work out, do they?"

Tommie's mouth dropped open. "What did you say?" she asked in a whisper.

"I guess I greased the cart before I bought the horse. Tommie Manning, will you marry me?"

She stood, leaned across the table, threw her arms around my neck and replied, "Yes! Yes I will, Joe Garth!"

We drove slowly back to the Manning's with Tommie's head on my shoulder, my right arm around her, and both off us looking at her left hand from time to time. After supper I'd taken Tommie to a jeweler's so that she could pick out a ring, and right there in the store I placed it on the third finger of her left hand. "If I'd known all it would take to get you to propose was to get stranded in Chickasha, I'd have done it a long time ago, Joe."

I chuckled. "Well, I've had it in mind for some time, but I wasn't too sure how you'd take it. I'm older than you, and I've got a few dollars right now, but basically I'm just a cowboy. Seems to me you could do a whole lot better."

It was Tommie's turn to laugh. "Oh, I don't know. My mother married a cowboy, and I don't think she ever regretted it. Of course, the manager of my department in Oklahoma City wants me to go out with him. He keeps sending me flowers and candy, but I guess he's going to be disappointed."

I gave her shoulders a shake in mock anger. "Don't you even speak to him when you pick up your last check."

CHAPTER FIFTEEN

When we told Tommie's folks about our engagement, they couldn't have been happier. Lillian kept asking me to bend down so she could kiss my cheek, and Fred pumped my hand until I thought it might fall off. I didn't know much about in-laws, though I'd heard the horror stories from some married friends, but none of those stories matched what was happening to me.

I called the ranch from the Manning's house and got a report from Roy that all was well. I told my foreman about the engagement, and Roy gave a loud cowboy whoop and said he would tell the other hands. Next, I called the house and told Rita the good news. She broke into excited Spanish, finally breaking back into English to ask if Tommie and I would be there for supper. The Manning's had already settled that question. Fred was in the kitchen with Lillian, and from the sounds of pots banging they were making a feast. I told Rita not tonight, but I wanted to plan an engagement party for the next weekend, and she and all of her clan would be invited. Rita hung up the phone with happy Spanish words floating through the air.

In May the wedding took place in the living room of my, soon to be our, house. Only close relatives and friends had been invited, and no press people, but still the house was filled. My friends from the Slash T, Handy Otler and Matt Walters and his wife were there, along with Miles Moore and his wife. It looked like Rita's entire family had come, which meant that there were little kids running around all over the place. Of course, Roy, Tom and Luke were up from the bunkhouse, along with Jose who was helping Rita in the kitchen.

The Garth family was not a large one. My sister, Janis, could not make the trip from San Francisco, and the only relatives I had in Texas were of the shirttail variety, second cousins and such. Some of them had contacted me to ask for money when they heard I'd won the lottery, but I managed to keep them at arms length.

Tommie's family was larger than mine, but only her parents and an aunt and uncle from each side were there. There had been a rift in the family in the distant past, and some didn't speak to others. Besides those folks, the only other people on Tommie's side of the aisle were two friends from her former job serving as attendants. Tommie had always wanted a small wedding, and I certainly didn't want any publicity, so everything worked out just right.

Rita's pastor, Rev. Carl Whiting, was going to preside. I'd called him soon after we were engaged, and he asked us to come to him for pre-marital counseling. We had gone to six sessions before Pastor Whiting agreed to officiate. He let us know that marriage was a sacred institution to him, and he did not marry couples just to legalize their union. One thing he required was an affirmation of faith from both parties, and that requirement led to some deep discussions about spiritual beliefs and personal faith.

Tommie had grown up attending a small church in the neighborhood, and I had a similar church background, but neither of us were happy with the traditional idea that a Christian must toe the party line of whatever denomination he or she belonged to. However, we both agreed that faith in Christ was a very personal aspect of our lives. At the end of the discussions, Pastor Whiting prayed with us and for us, suggesting that we maintain an open dialog about faith in our marriage. Over the weeks of meeting with him, both of us had come to like and respect this quiet unassuming man with so much spiritual steel in his character.

It was 2:00 p.m. when one of Rita's daughters began to play the wedding march on a keyboard rented for the occasion. Handy, my best man, and I were standing in front of the fireplace, both of us feeling somewhat uncomfortable in dark suits. Pastor Whiting was standing a step in front of us looking down the aisle created by rows of rented chairs.

Lillian Manning was on the bride's side in her wheelchair watching with a glow of pride as her lovely daughter came floating slowly down the aisle on her father's arm. Her dress was magnificent and traditional, white with a long sweeping train and lace half sleeves down her arms ending in a point on the back of her hands. A lace and gauze veil covered her pretty face.

"Dearly beloved, we are gathered here in the sight of God

and this congregation to unite Joe and Tommie in holy matrimony," the minister began. I was looking at this beautiful girl standing beside me, wondering at the miracle that had brought us to this point, and I had tuned Pastor Whiting out until I realized from the silence that I was supposed to respond. There were chuckles in the crowd as I turned my head and looked blankly at the minister, who repeated, "Joe, do you take Tommie to be your wedded wife? To ...." The ceremony went on, and finally I heard the words, "I now pronounce you man and wife: you may kiss the bride." I flipped the veil up and gave Tommie a resounding kiss to the applause of all the spectators.

When the reception was over, we drove away in the pickup, trailing a long line of cans that the hands had tied to the bumper. We dragged them all the way to the gate, and then I got out and cut them loose, leaving the whole mess there for Tom to pick up.

I'd told Tommie that we would go anywhere she wanted for a honeymoon, and she'd chosen a cruise in the Gulf of Mexico. We left the pickup at Wichita Falls Regional airport and flew to Galveston.

After two days on the cruise ship, we were both totally bored with it. We liked to dance, and the food was good, but when we booked the trip we didn't know that the ship was a floating casino. Not only did we not like to gamble; we found that most of the other passengers had little interest in anything else. The ship sailed down into the Gulf, and then turned and headed back to New Orleans. It was to lie off the Big Easy for a day, and then go back into the Gulf, but Tommie and I decided we'd had enough cruising, and we got off at New Orleans and flew back home.

Now things settled into a happy, pleasant routine for me. My life had changed so much in the last year that I hardly recognized myself. Tommie, a homemaker and rancher's wife at heart, was delighted to be in charge of the house, and she and Rita worked smoothly together.

The ranch was doing well, with Black Angus calves growing fast and the mares all safely in foal. I had a monthly report from Duckworth, and I did notice that my bank balance was still steadily decreasing, but that didn't disturb me much. As soon as I started selling calves I would put some money back in.

By the end of August, Tommie was sure that she was pregnant, and she and Rita began decorating a small bedroom as a nursery. I couldn't imagine what it would be like to be a father, but somewhat to my surprise I was really looking forward to it.

One Saturday morning Tommie and I were having coffee out on the back deck, watching the cows and calves in the north pasture, when the phone rang and Rita came to say that Miles Moore was on the line. "Hey, Miles," Joe said. "When are you coming out to see us?"

"Soon, Joe, real soon. But today I've got a fellow here in my office I'd like you to talk to. His name is Howard Reagan, and he's in the oil business. Okay if I put him on?"

"Sure, Miles."

"Mr. Garth, thanks for talking to me. I'm a driller, and I've got a well spudded in down by Bowie. We're down about three thousand feet, and there are good indicators of oil and gas, but the man who was my venture capitalist died last week, and his estate has shut off the money. I'm looking for someone to invest in finishing the well for a 1/16 share. Would you be interested?"

"Well, Mr. Reagan, I don't know anything at all about oil or oil wells, and I kind of make it a rule to never invest in things I don't know about."

"Miles told me about that, Mr. Garth, but I would sure like the opportunity to show you what I've got. I can also give you several references so you can find out about me."

"Hmm. Please put Miles back on the phone, Mr. Reagan." There was a pause, and then Miles said, "Yes, Joe."

"Miles, I know this guy's right there close, so I'll ask some questions and you just answer yes or no, okay?"

"Yes."

"Have you known Reagan long?"

"Yes."

"Over five years?"

"No.

"Does he have a good reputation?"

"Yes. Pretty good."

"Are you recommending him?"

"Yes, I am, with reservations."

"Thanks Miles. I understand. Put him back on the phone."

"Mr. Reagan," I said, "I'll take a look at what you've got, but no guarantees. Can you come out here this afternoon?"

"Yes, sir, I can. What time?"

"Let's say 2:00 p.m."

"Thanks, Mr. Garth. I'll see you at two."

Tommie had been listening to my side of the conversation, and when I hung up she asked, "What was that all about?"

"Oh, Miles has recommended an oilman to me. He's going to come out to show us what he has. Wants me to invest in his drilling operation."

"Do you know anything about investing in oil wells?"

"Not a thing," I replied. "However, I didn't know anything about being married either until you came along. I'm not doing too bad, am I?"

Tommie laughed and got up to hug me. "No, dear, you're not doing too bad. If you are as successful with oil wells as you are in the husband department, I think you'll do all right"

I kissed her. "Heck of a note when a man has to fish for compliments," I said, and then continued, "But you know, Tommie, the money won't last forever, and we've got a baby to think about. Some royalty checks will sure help with his education, don't you think?"

"Oh, yes. But what makes you think we're going to have a boy? Wouldn't you like to have a little girl?"

"Honey, I'll take whatever you give me. A daughter as pretty as you wouldn't hurt my feelings a bit."

At two o'clock on the dot Howard Reagan rang the front

doorbell. Rita showed him into my office, and left to get coffee. I introduced Tommie, and we all sat down in easy chairs around a coffee table. The office was spacious and well decorated with Charles Russell prints of western scenes on the walls, a wedding gift from Tommie. My desk was in an alcove with large windows that looked out on the horse and cow barns, and across from it was a long conference table.

"Well, Mr. Reagan, tell us what you have in mind," I said.

"Could I spread some things out on the table over there?" the oilman asked.

I nodded and got up to follow the man over to the table where he spread out some maps and cost sheets. Reagan began to show us where the drilling was taking place. "If we bring this well in, I've got a two-year lease on 80 acres, and I plan to drill at least two more wells, maybe three."

He pointed to a red X on the map. "Here's the well we're drilling right now. As I told you on the phone, we're down to three thousand feet and the indicators look good. Do you know anything about oil bearing strata, Mr. Garth?"

"I don't know anything about oil drilling at all, Howard. There's really no need to explain all the terms to me. If this well comes in, and we have a $1/16^{th}$ share, how much will that return?"

"Well, the price of oil at the well head will determine the actual price, but at today's prices if we pump 50 barrels a day, and that's conservative, your share would run about $86.00 a day. That's $31,390.00 a year. That's a 6.2% return on your investment of five hundred thousand."

I did some calculations with a pencil. "At that rate, it would take about fifteen years to pay back my original investment. Somehow that doesn't seem all that rosy. What else do you have?"

Reagan beamed. He seemed to know he had me on the hook, and he was right. I had a hunch that this could be a very good investment. "Ah, but for $500,000.00 you also get options on the rest of the lease. That means that you have the right to invest in the other wells drilled at the same 1/16th return."

Tommie had been quiet to this point, but now she spoke up. "Mr. Reagan, I don't know much about oil either, but what if Joe invests in this well you're drilling, and you don't find oil? What happens to the five hundred thousand then?"

"I'm glad you asked that question, Mrs. Garth," he said, though the look on his face was kind of pinched, and I had a hunch he was *not glad at all* that she'd asked the question. "What you have then is a great tax loss. I'm sure your accountant can tell you about that, but if you are paying high taxes, a significant tax loss can save you money in the end. And then there are the federal payments that come to drillers if they fail to bring in a well. I won't go into all of the ins and outs, but you can receive a substantial portion of your investment back in tax-free payments from Uncle Sam. Right now the federal government is anxious to have drillers explore for oil, and they're bending over backwards to help us out."

The discussion went on until I finally told Reagan that we would come out and look at the well, and then decide whether or not to invest. The driller would obviously rather have had an answer right then, but he seemed to know better than to push any harder, so he agreed. He gave us a copy of a location map and told us how to follow it to the well, and then he left.

When we were alone again, I asked Tommie what she thought. "Joe, the money you have is yours, and I don't intend to tell you how to spend it, but from everything I hear oil drilling is a risky business. Do you think you should ask someone who knows the oil business for advice?"

"That's not a bad idea, Tommie. And by the way, the money is ours, not mine. Do you know anybody to ask?"

"No, but I'll bet your accountant would know someone. Why don't you ask him?"

I called Duckworth and asked if he could recommend anyone, and the accountant said he would get back to me. In an hour I was talking to Harold Farmer on the phone. Farmer was from an old oil family, stretching back to the oil boom in the 1920's. He knew Howard Reagan, and didn't have anything really bad to say about him, but he urged caution. Wildcatters rarely told all of the facts about any well they wanted someone to invest in. He gave me some questions to ask, and told me what to look for in the slush pit. I thanked him and rang off.

The next afternoon we followed the map Reagan had given us and finally came to the drilling rig. We stopped a good way back, but the driller had been watching for us, and he came walking across the dusty pasture to the pickup. Reagan looked like an oilman with his oil-spotted clothes and silver hardhat. He stopped beside my open window and said, "I won't shake hands, Mr. Garth, because you don't want yours dirty. As you can see, the day tower is working, and we're down another five hundred feet. If you want to come closer, I'll show you around, though not up on the drilling floor. It's way to dangerous to have visitors up there."

On Mr. Farmer's advice Tommie and I had come dressed in old clothes and boots prepared to look at the works. We followed Reagan over to a low-bermed pit filled with bad-smelling water and oil. "Here's the latest stuff we've pulled up," Reagan said as he squatted down and crumbled some clay in his hands. "See these streaks here? That's the indicator. I think we'll hit oil in another five hundred to a thousand feet." The streaks *did* look like those Farmer had told me about.

Again we followed as the driller moved around the high platform where the drilling was going on. The noise of the huge diesel engine and the clanging of pipe against the tower stand were constant, and almost made it impossible to hear. Reagan pointed to things and shouted words only half heard. Finally, we moved back to the pickup, and I said, "Can you show us some other areas on the lease where you intend to drill?"

"Sure thing. Why don't I get my pickup and you follow me?"

We bumped over rough pasture, seeing a few Hereford cows in the distance. The driller showed us three other locations, but the ground all looked the same to Tommie and me.

Finally, we stopped on the road back to the gate. As we got out, I asked one of the questions Mr. Farmer had suggested. "In the past five years, how many wells have you brought in, Mr. Reagan?"

"Nine," the oilman replied. "And they're all still pumping. I can show you some of them if you want."

"Maybe later," I replied. "Over all, what's your drilling cost per barrel?"

"I see you've been doing your homework, Mr. Garth. That's good. I want you to ask all the questions you can. Right now my average drilling cost is $15.00 a barrel. Now that's kind of deceptive. That average goes back over twenty years, and in a lot of those years oil was selling for less than $10.00 a barrel. If this well we're working on comes in, with increased costs in today's market, the drilling cost will be about $20.00 a barrel."

After a few more questions, which Howard Reagan was quick to answer, I said we'd let the man know the next day, and we drove off the lease.

Tommie and I discussed what we'd seen and heard all the way back to the ranch. We agreed that most of the things Reagan and told us seemed on the up and up, and the next morning I called Harold Farmer again and told him what we had found out. Farmer was very helpful. "Well, Mr. Garth, I think Howard Reagan is living up to the wildcatter's reputation. I have no idea whether or not he will bring the well in he's drilling, but with the answers he's given you, I'd say he has a good chance."

"Thank you, Mr. Farmer. If you tell me what I owe you, I'll send you a check for consulting."

Farmer laughed. "There's no charge, Mr. Garth. Some day I might need some advice on cattle or horses, and I'll call you."

"Any time, sir. Any time."

After talking further, we decided to take the plunge and invest in Mr. Reagan's well. The deciding factor was the possibility of royalties that would set up a nice college fund for Junior or Jane.

I called Howard Reagan and told him to have the paperwork drawn up. We would sign everything at our bank and transfer the money at that time.

CHAPTER SIXTEEN

Hot summer settled down as it always does in Texas. Everyone looked forward to the infrequent thunderstorms that brought a lot of excitement and at least a momentary relief from the 100-degree days, but no one wanted to see tornado clouds forming. The devastation of the huge 1979 twister that tore through southwest Wichita Falls was still fresh in the minds of those who had lived through it.

I was planning a calf sale for late fall, and I had workmen building an open-sided sale barn south of the cattle pens. Tommie was happy in her early pregnancy, and I surprised myself by becoming more delighted all the time with the prospect of being a father.

Tommie sold her little red car, and I bought her a Ford Expedition as a belated wedding present. I didn't want to cut off Tommie's mobility, but I wanted a safer bunch of metal surrounding her and the baby in their travels, and I felt better about her being in the big Expedition.

Everything seemed to be going so well, that it was a surprise when Tommie woke me up one night with panic in her voice. *"Joe! I'm hurting awfully bad! I think I need a doctor!"*

We rushed to the hospital, and I walked back and forth in the waiting room until a green-clad doctor came out to tell me that Tommie had miscarried, but she would be all right. He let me go in to see her even though she was still groggy from anesthetic. She looked so small in the hospital bed, and when I spoke her name and leaned over to kiss her, she began to weep. "I'm so sorry, Joe. So sorry," she said.

Mustering up a smile, I replied, "You don't have a thing to be sorry about. The doctor told me that these things happen, but it's sure not your fault. You just rest easy, now. I love you very much, and I was afraid I would lose you." A tear trickled down her cheek and I reached out to brush it away, and then sat down beside her and held her hand until a nurse came in to shoo me away.

It was just after daylight when I called Tommie's folks, catching Fred as he was going out to feed. Fred said he would tell Lillian, and they would call later to see when was a good time to visit Tommie. Next I called Rita and asked her to pass the word to Roy and the crew. And then I sat down in the waiting room to do the only thing I could do – wait. Fred and Lillian came in the afternoon, and Tommie was feeling well enough to sit up and visit with them, though she was still very weak.

The doctor kept Tommie in the hospital overnight, and I stayed with her, though she told me to go home and get some rest. "I sure wouldn't rest at home with you in here," I replied, and stayed anyway. I'd loved her before the miscarriage, but I'd taken her for granted, and in that long night I saw how much this lovely girl really meant to me; how much she had changed my life. It was as if I had only been half alive until we married. The thought of almost losing her was a very painful one.

Tommie was released the next morning, and I took her home. Of course, when I carried her through the front door at home, over her protest, Rita was waiting to take over. Tommie's mom and dad came right over to see her when I called to let them know we were home, and they stayed for lunch.

Two days later I took Tommie back to the doctor for a checkup. "Do you know what caused me to miscarry?" Tommie asked him.

"It could have been a lot of things, Mrs. Garth. You're healthy and young, and I don't see any specific reason. Sometimes the body just decides to expel a fetus for no apparent reason. I think that's what happened in your case."

"Will I still be able to have children?"

"I don't see why not. No major damage was done, and you'll heal quickly. Why don't you make an appointment to come back in two weeks and I'll check you again, just to make sure."

On the way home, we talked about trying again, since we both wanted children, but I was cautious because I didn't want anything to endanger Tommie's life. "Let's wait until we're sure you're back to normal, Tommie. I want a baby, but I sure don't want anything to happen to you."

Tommie hugged my arm and replied, "That's nice to hear, and we'll wait a while, but not too long. After all, Rita and I have the baby's room all decorated, and we wouldn't want it to go to waste."

Summer moved into fall and the heat abated somewhat. The Angus calves were all large now, and the new sale barn was completed. I planned to hold the auction in November to sell the calves. In August the cows and calves had been separated for weaning, and so that the young bulls would not be running with the heifers. Some bulls and heifers became fertile very young, and I didn't want to take any chances. Of course, the cows were all safely with calf again as the herd sires had been running with them from June until August.

The four beautiful King Ranch mares were now heavy with foal to Handy's Own and due to drop their babies early in the year, and Tommie and I were really looking forward to that.

One day in October I saddled Buck and Tommie's quiet gelding Dusty, and we went for a ride to the south pasture. It was a lovely fall day, the temperature just right with a soft southwest breeze blowing gently across the grassy pastures.

"You know, Tommie," I said. "A year ago I was working at the Slash T, and we had an early blue norther when we were gathering cattle. I remember thinking that if I ever had any money I'd make sure somebody else had to climb into a cold saddle and chase cows on a day when all sensible people were sitting by the fire. It was not long after that I heard I'd won the lottery. Things sure have changed in one year. Now I've got this place, and some hands working for me, in case anybody has to chase cows in the next norther, and best of all I found you along the road. A man's life doesn't get much better than this, does it?"

Tommie laughed. "And not only that, but look how fat Buck's getting. It seems to me that he's taken to the rich man's life as well as you have."

I grinned and patted the horse on the neck. "You mean we're both fat and happy?"

"Well, you're not fat, but you do seem to be happy. Want to know something else?"

"Sure. Go ahead and make my day."

"I'm pregnant again. I tested last night, and it was positive."

I pulled Buck close to Dusty and reached out to give Tommie a big shoulder hug. "I thought so," I replied.

"What do you mean you thought so?"

I chuckled. "Well, now, I don't know much about pregnant women, but I've seen a lot of first calf heifers in my time, and there's just a certain look they all get…"

Tommie pulled off her hat and batted me with it. "A heifer!" she cried. "You're comparing me to a cow?"

"A *real pretty* heifer, of course."

She settled down, allowing that maybe *that* was okay, and we went on with our ride, happy and satisfied with each other.

Almost before I could blink, two good things happened in succession. Howard Reagan called to say the well had come in, and it looked like a good one, and I received a letter from one of the best auctioneers in the area saying he would be available for the calf auction.

When the calf sale was over, I could expect to put some money in the bank instead of taking it out as I'd been doing. I called Harold Duckworth and asked him for a statement of account. "Harold, please do an audit and let me know how much is going out each month. Take a good look at the main bank account and tell me if we could do better somewhere else."

"Sure thing, Mr. Garth. I've got most of the figures right here, but I'll put it all together and give you a call."

Later, Duckworth called and gave me the figures, and they were a bit disturbing; the balance was just over one million. I showed the figures to Tommie, and she asked if we needed to cut back on spending, but I assured her we would be all right. "When I was working at the Slash T I never thought I'd have one thousand dollars in the bank, Tommie, so a million is still a bit beyond my figuring. Anyway, we'll have some money coming from the oil well, and the sale of our calves pretty soon, so it isn't all outgo anymore."

The calf sale came, and since I had, at the advice of another Angus breeder, advertised in farm magazines and ranch papers, plus on TV and major newspapers, there was a big crowd right from the start. Taking a page out of the King Ranch's book, I had Jose and Tom dig a pit in back of the bunkhouse to bury a barbequed beef. This had been advertised with the sale, and a lot of local ranchers had turned up to buy calves and eat beef. The meal would take place at noon, followed by the sale at 1:00 p.m.

November weather in North Texas can be suddenly changeable, so preparations were made to serve the food indoors in case of rain or a norther, but in fact it was a clear day with temperatures in the seventies. The auctioneer arrived at 8:00 a.m. to set up his equipment and supervise sorting the cattle. Elmer Hutchins had the reputation of running the best livestock auctions in our part of the state, and as I watched him work, I could see why. No detail was too small for him, and before long he had things well in hand.

Guests and buyers began to arrive at nine o'clock, and the parking area, a designated strip of pasture, was soon filling up with cars and pickups. Several ranchers brought trailers with them, a good sign. They were parked near the sale arena.

Tommie and I were as busy as cats on a hot tin roof. I was handling the livestock questions and the cowboys hired for the event, and Tommie was supervising all cooking and eating arrangements, as well as making sure the female guests were comfortable. The men had restroom facilities at the barns and bunkhouse, but a guest bathroom in the main house had been set aside for the ladies.

At eleven thirty Jose and two helpers dug up the side of beef and laid it on a large trestle table. They unwrapped the burlap and revealed the steaming meat and a wonderful aroma. Jose carved large patters full and set them on the tables, and then stood by to take special orders. The four teenage boys hired as waiters moved at a run, making sure the china plates were available and filling iced tea glasses and coffee cups.

Tommie and I came together under the portico next to

the horse barn before we went to get our plates. "Joe, this is a lot of hard work, but it's sure a lot fun. Do you see that short man in the big gray hat sitting over by the chinaberry tree? He took two plates, both heaped high with beef. No potato salad, no beans, no bread, just beef. He's sitting over there at the table right now eating as fast as he can."

I laughed out loud. "That's Alex Campbell, babe. He never misses a cattle sale or a free meal, and if he can get them together, so much the better. Old Alex is famous around this part of the country for the amount of food he can put away. But this is the main thing: he's also a buyer for the Circle H Ranch & Feedlots. The Circle H is owned by Elroy Masterson, a rich recluse who has ranches spread all over the country, though most people don't know that. The story is if Alex likes the food, he'll buy, if not, he leaves before the sale starts."

"Well, from the looks of things, I think he'll be here when we start selling. He's going back for seconds, or fourths, right now." We watched as the cattle buyer went over to Jose and pointed where he wanted him to cut.

"I reckon we better get our plates, Tommie, before Alex comes back again. I'd hate to have to eat peanut butter and jelly sandwiches at my own barbeque."

"I don't think there's any danger of that, dear. And by the way, Rita will be down soon with her girls bringing the best peach cobbler in the world for dessert."

Sure enough, just as we moved to the table, Rita and two of her daughters came down the path from the house carrying large covered baking pans and surrounded by the wonderful aroma of peach cobbler. Murmurs ran through the crowd as the three ladies sat the pans down and whipped off the lids. They were immediately welcomed with rousing applause as the guests descended on the cobbler.

When the meal was finally over, Jose and his helpers began cleaning up as the well-filled men and women made their way to the sales arena. I gave a signal to Roy, who in turn said to the men on horseback in the large pens, "Bring 'em on, boys."

The auctioneer began his spiel and the first of the fine Black Angus heifers entered the ring, heads up and feet prancing. The final count for our forty cows had been 22 females and 18 bull calves. One after the other they went under the hammer for premium prices. Alex Campbell bought three bulls for his boss, and the rest went to different individuals.

As cattle sales went this was not a large offering, but the calves were in top condition, and there were many favorable comments. I began right then planning to buy more cows and have a bigger sale the next year.

To top the day off, I appeared at the end of the sale riding Handy's Own followed by his harem of fine brood mares. As we loped around the arena to the applause of the crowd, the auctioneer said, "Look at that horseflesh! Folks, next year Joe and Tommie Garth will be selling the foals by this great King Ranch stallion *Handy's Own*, out of these fine King Ranch mares. You will all receive a notice of the sale." As I waved my hat in the air and rode back toward the horse barn, the announcer continued, "Oh, yes. Joe wanted me to tell you that at the horse sale there will be another barbequed beef! And more peach cobbler!" The crowd applauded even louder and yelled their pleasure.

When the last of the guests was gone, Tommie and I watched as stock trailers backed up to the chutes to load the calves, and Brittany Saint, my bookkeeper, collected the checks. All in all it had been a very successful day. "Let's celebrate by taking your folks out to dinner, babe," I said.

"Great idea, Joe. You know they were here for just a bit before lunch, and Rita sent them off with huge plates full of beef and cobbler. I'll give them a call and see if they're up to a night on the town."

I watched her walk back up the path to the house thinking how lucky I was to have this lovely girl in my life.

CHAPTER SEVENTEEN

December came in with a blast of arctic air that swept down across North Texas like a chilling scythe. From six in the morning until five in the afternoon the temperature dropped 35 degrees. I was down at the barns with the hands all day making sure the livestock was taken care of. The cattle had been moved up from the south pasture before the calf sale, and they were pastured close enough to the loafing sheds that they had plenty of shelter. Cattle can stand a lot of cold, but a steady freezing wind chill with no shelter will mean losses. The horses were safely in their barn, Handy's Own in his large loose stall, the mares clustered together in a pen on the south side of the barn, and the saddle stock in the big corral beside them. There were warm open-faced sheds in both of these pens.

The key in cold weather for horses and cattle is to make plenty of high protein feed and windbreaks available. We had cut some good Coastal Bermuda hay on our own place, and I bought more in large round bales, each weighing some twelve hundred pounds. Some of these bales were spotted in the cow pastures in hay rings, hauled out by Tom on the tractor with a fork on both ends. The large bales made good windbreaks for the cattle, and many of the cows seemed as comfortable sheltering behind the hay bales as those who came into the loafing shed.

The horse barn had a large hay storage area, and it was filled with a combination of coastal hay and alfalfa. In warm weather very little alfalfa was fed as it was far too high in protein for horses that were not working every day, but in cold weather, each horse got a portion of alfalfa along with grass hay to boost their body heat. That, along with the sweet feed they received twice a day kept them in good shape.

By the time darkness spread across the ranch, all the animals were taken care of, supper was over, and I was seated with Tommie on the love seat in front of a roaring log fire. Rita finished up her chores and retired to her quarters with a cheery, "Buenos notches," and the house was quiet, the only sound the wind humming around the eaves and quiet music playing on the stereo.

"When I was a little girl, I always liked it when the northers blew at night," Tommie said. "I would snuggle down in my bed and feel all warm and safe."

I pulled her closer. "When I was a kid, my folks rented a little two by four place down south of Olney, and usually we didn't have enough feed or shelter for our cattle, so when the northers blew me and my brother would have to build brush shelters along the fence lines and haul feed out to the animals with a tractor and wagon. I can remember being rousted out of bed long before daylight by Dad when a wind like this one blew. Sometimes we'd work for twenty hours at a stretch and still lose cattle."

Tommie leaned back and looked at me in amazement. "I didn't know you had a brother," she said. "Where does he live?"

"He's dead, Tommie. Killed in the Gulf War. Sorry I've never mentioned him to you, but I don't like to think or talk about Richie much. Of course, you know both of my folks died in that car crash on Highway 79 ten years ago. That was right after we heard about Richie." I hugged her tighter. "So, except for Janis out in California, you and Pete, here," I patted her stomach, "are the only close kin I have."

"I'm sorry about your brother and your folks, Joe, but Pete and I will try to fill all the gaps we can."

And then it was suddenly Christmas time. In celebration of the holiday, Tommie and I wanted to have a party for the ranch people, Rita's family, and Tommie's folks. We called it a *family* party, and we meant it just that way. Rita was totally excited, and she and Tommie spent days decorating the house. Roy and I went into town and found a huge Douglas fir hauled in from Colorado, and when we had it set up in the den under the point of the cathedral ceiling it looked great.

"You know, babe, we ought to get used to having kids around," I said to Tommie one morning. "Why don't we ask Rita's grandchildren to trim the tree?"

"That's a great idea," Tommie replied. "I'll see what Rita thinks, and if she approves, I'll go pick them all up this afternoon." Rita also thought it was a fine idea, and she and Tommie started phoning the family right away.

By 2:00 p.m. the house was filled with children's voices and Christmas ornaments. Rita made spice tea and cocoa, and the kids were almost too excited to stand still. Tommie and I tried to supervise, but the tree took on a different appearance than we had anticipated. Because the oldest child was fourteen-year-old Angelina, only five-feet tall, there were no decorations and few icicles above the highest point she could reach, though the kids had thrown icicles and tinsel as high as they could get them.

I got out a short ladder and more decorations began to appear in the higher branches balancing things out a bit. And then a magical moment came when Angelina said, "Uncle Joe, Madeline is the smallest one of us. In our house the smallest one is always lifted up to place the angel on the top. Could we do that here?"

I had a bit of a lump in my throat as I looked down at delicate Madeline. She was just four, and her face was shining like a star. I picked her up and held her tight, and Angelina gave her the pretty white angel with wings made of real feathers. I stepped up on the ladder, holding the little girl high so she could place the angel on top of the tree, and when it was done, leaning down slightly as if ready to announce the birth of the Christ Child, I stepped back down and held onto Madeline as all the children sang "Silent Night" in Spanish and English.

I sat down in a chair still holding the little girl, and Tommie stood behind me with her hands on my shoulders. The rest of the children just naturally sat on the floor in a semicircle in front of me, and Angelina asked, "Uncle Joe, will you tell us a story?"

A story, huh? I thought for a minute, and then began: "Well, it was a cold day, kind of like today, only there was a lot of snow for this story took place up north where the snow gets really deep. The house wasn't very nice, and it was too small for all the children that filled it, but it was a happy house. Dad worked at a feed store, and he didn't make much money, and Mom took care of the children at home, and tried to help out the finances by baking bread and rolls for people.

"Christmas was coming, and Mom and Dad were trying to

come up with presents for all the kids. Dad was a good wood carver, and he had made some wooden cars and things for the four boys, and Mom had sewn up some new dresses and such for the three older girls, and made cloth dolls, but they wanted something more for their kids. Of course, the baby wasn't yet a year old, so the new doll Mom made for her out of a sock would be fine."

All of the older kids were listening intently to the story, and they called out together, "What's the baby's name?"

I grinned, and replied, "Why, the baby's name is Madeline, of course," and the little girl on my lap wriggled with pleasure and snuggled closer.

"Anyway, it looked like it would be a cold, white Christmas, and since the house was heated by a coal stove, what extra money the family had would have to go for coal.

"Then, just two days before Christmas, a terrible thing happened. Mom walked down town like she always did to get some ground beef, Black Angus, of course, and as she turned the corner on the slippery sidewalk on her way back home, she slipped and fell. Luckily, she did not have baby Madeline with her, as she had left the baby with the older children, but she was hurt bad. Two people in a nearby car had seen Mom fall, and they went to help her. The man said, 'I'm sorry, ma'am, but it looks like your leg is broken.'

"They helped her into their car and quickly drove her to the hospital where her leg was x-rayed. Sure enough, it was broken. As soon as she could she called the feed store and told Dad about her leg. Of course, they didn't have a phone at home, so Dad left work and walked home to tell the children, and then on to the hospital to be with Mom. The cast on her leg was dry and hard, so the doctor said she could go home. Dad and Mom didn't have any health insurance, so Dad signed a paper agreeing to pay the bill a little at a time.

"Since the family didn't have a car, Dad called his boss, a nice man, to ask if he could take Mom home in his car. When Dad helped Mom out of the car at home, all of the kids ran out to meet her.

"Well, the next day was Christmas Eve, and since the kids were home for Christmas vacation, they took care of Mom and the baby. Dad only worked half a day, and then he was home, too. Soon everybody was busy wrapping gifts for each other. Once the gifts were wrapped, they put them under the tree. Like I said, it was a happy house, even though Mom's broken leg kind of made them sad.

"That night when all the children were finally asleep, Dad hung their stockings up on the wall near the stove. Each stocking held an apple and a piece of hard candy, except for Madeline's. There was a new bib and a soft toy Mom had sewn up in hers. Then he banked the fire, and they went to bed.

"Way after midnight Dad heard some slight noises in the living room, but he just figured it was one of the kids who couldn't wait, so he rolled over and went back to sleep.

"Early the next morning the kids all rushed into their parents' bedroom and woke them up with loud cries. 'Mom! Dad! Come see what we got!' Madeline woke up and the oldest girl picked her up out of her crib and took her out to the tree. When Dad helped Mom out to the living room they saw a small mountain of packages under, around and beside the small Christmas tree. And the stockings were bulging with gifts.

"Dad and Mom were amazed. Where had all of these things come from? The kids didn't ask any questions though; they were too busy tearing off wrapping paper and opening boxes. Soon there were new dolls and toy trains scattered among trucks and artists' sets. As their folks looked on quietly talking about how these things came to be, the kids finally came to the bottom of the pile. There, under all the other gifts were the things Mom and Dad had made for them. And right beside those gifts were the things the children had made for each other and their parents.

"Well, it was kind of quiet now as they all opened these final gifts. All the kids hugged Mom and Dad and Madeline, who was sitting on Mom's lap holding the soft toy horse Mom had made her. Everybody thanked everybody else, and the kids went back to playing with their new toys.

"Mom said, 'Now that the excitement is over, I better start cooking.' Dad helped her into the kitchen and said he would be her arms and legs if she would tell him what to do. He opened the door of the refrigerator to get out the chicken that Mom was going to roast for Christmas dinner – they couldn't afford a turkey or a ham – but the chicken had been replaced by a huge turkey! 'Where did this come from?' Mom asked. 'I guess the same place all those gifts came from,' Dad replied, and they looked at each other with amazed looks on their faces.

"It turned out to be a really great Christmas, with lots of food and happiness all around. And when Dad went out to get some more fuel for the stove, he discovered that the shed was full of coal! There was enough coal to last the rest of the winter.

"Dad and Mom spent a lot of time that day trying to figure out where all of those wonderful things came from, but they didn't have any luck at all. What do you think?"

The kids began to shout their answers: "Santa Claus!" "Jesus!" "The Heavenly Father!" "Dad's boss!" "The doctor at the hospital!" and on and on.

Finally, Tommie, who along with Rita had listened to the story, said, "Okay, Mister Storyteller. Where *did* all those things come from?" But I just smiled and shook my head as if I didn't know either.

That evening when all the kids had gone back home and we were once again snuggled up on the couch in front of the fire, Tommie said, "That was a wonderful story you told the kids this afternoon. Where did it come from?"

I laughed. "Maybe it really happened, or maybe I just made it up. What do you think?"

"I think you're not going to tell me, and that's fine. I like a little mystery in my man. And I liked the way you treated the kids today, it shows what a good father you're going to be. Wasn't that little Madeline the sweetest thing you've ever seen?"

I squeezed her tight. "Yes, she was. All the kids were great. I kept thinking that we should make this an annual event, and before long our own boy or girl will be right in the middle of them."

The fire burned down, but Tommie and I had long since sought our warm bed. Just before she drifted off to sleep, Tommie whispered in my ear, "I'm so lucky to be married to you, Joe."

CHAPTER EIGHTEEN

The Christmas party on the Saturday before Christmas was a huge success. As soon as it was going well, Tommie and I brought out boxes of gifts for the kids, and soon the house was filled with torn wrapping paper and excited voices.

As usual, the men and women split into groups, and all of the men wanted to see the horses and cattle, so we put on coats and left the women clustered in the kitchen chattering away in two languages, and the children making lots of noise with their new toys.

Noon came and the table was groaning with food. Tommie and Rita had baked and cooked for days before the party, and it seemed that all of the other women had brought at least one dish, so there was plenty of food. It was hard to get the children to settle down enough to eat, but finally they were more or less quiet, and I asked the blessing, somewhat self-consciously.

When the meal was over and the dishes were taken care of, I announced that I had a surprise for everyone, even Tommie. "Now, we've all had plenty to eat, and we'll be having more in the days to come, but not everyone is as fortunate as we are. So, last week I asked Pastor Whiting what the best way was to help the needy in Wichita Falls. He put me in touch with Major Gatling at the Salvation Army, and we arranged for something special. This only applies to those who want to take part, but at 5:00 p.m. today we're going in to the Salvation Army kitchen behind the old library building and serve food to the people gathered there."

The room was totally silent as I finished my speech. Then, Max Blanco, Rita's oldest son, said, "Dad would have loved this, Joe. He was always doing something at that shelter. I'm with you," and a chorus of voices rose to shout out their willingness to come along.

Tommie came over and stood on tiptoe to kiss me. She didn't say anything, but her eyes were filled with tears and love. Rita was crying openly at Max's reminder of her late husband's love for his fellow human beings.

Fred and Lillian both told me what a great idea it was, and Fred gave me a check to pass along to the Major, saying that he and Lillian would not try to make the trip, but they would be along in spirit. I bent down and gave my mother-in-law a kiss on the cheek and shook Fred's hand, and then I took Fred aside and told him what else I'd done, and Fred said he would tell Lillian on their way home.

The caravan of cars and pickups stretched for a long way as I led them into the city. I was driving Tommie's Expedition, and it was filled with kids singing Christmas Carols. Once we arrived at the Salvation Army shelter, and all the cars had emptied, I led them in. We were met by Major Gatling, who quickly appointed jobs for each one, making sure that the children were paired with an adult to help serve.

It was a wonderful way to end a perfect day. The food was good and plentiful, and the people we served were thankful and appreciative. The afternoon passed quickly, and it was almost nine o'clock when we pointed the Expedition's nose toward the ranch. Tommie took hold of my right hand, leaving my left free for driving, and said, "What a wonderful surprise that was, Joe Garth. I don't know when I've felt so good. Do we need to send the shelter some more food?"

I grinned. "That's all taken care of. After I first spoke to the major I set up a trust for the shelter through Duckworth. Also, today's meal was donated to the shelter in honor of Fred and Lillian Manning. I know they wanted to come with us, but your mother looked pretty tired, and I told Fred what I'd done so he could share it with her after they got home."

Tommie smiled. "I do believe you've won every Manning heart in Texas, Joe; is there any way that this Manning can show you how much I love you?"

I smiled down at her. "Oh, I'll think of something. Anyway, babe, I owe your parents a big debt, one I'll never be able to repay. You're the best thing that ever happened in my life, Tommie Garth, and I don't think I can ever show you how much you mean to me. When we're as old as your mom and dad, I want us to be as close as they are to each other. So stick around, Tommie Manning Garth. I sure don't want to lose you."

Tommie leaned over and kissed my cheek. "I'm not going anywhere that you won't be able to find me, Joe. You couldn't lose me if you wanted to." We continued on home in warm, comfortable silence.

CHAPTER NINETEEN

Christmas day was wonderful, sort of a continuation of the party feeling from Saturday. The weather was warm and sunny, and everyone was in the Christmas spirit. Rita had invited us to an early Christmas service at her church, and we accepted her invitation. I'd attended the Chapel of Grace several times after my first visit, and after I met Tommie she had gone with me, and we always enjoyed the services.

We sat with Rita and her family, and when little Madeline, in her starched white Christmas dress, saw me sit down, she pushed through the other children and crawled up on my knee to give me a big hug. Then she planted herself on my lap in a proprietary way for the rest of the service. It was a strange and wonderful feeling to have the child there, and I thought how much I was looking forward to holding our baby when the time came.

When we got home, Tommie went to work on the Christmas dinner she and Rita had put together over the past few days. Of course, Rita was with her family on this special day, but Tommie enjoyed serving dinner for us and her parents, who would join us.

While Tommie worked on the meal, I went down to the barns to take care of the animals. I'd given the hands several days off, and they were all gone. Roy had a sister in Wichita Falls, and he was going there for dinner, but he told me he'd be back later in the afternoon and take care of the evening chores. Roy's real home was on the ranch, and he treated the animals as if they were his own.

Dinner was a great success, and Tommie glowed under our complements. When her folks left to go home, she said, "Can we have a Christmas like this one every year? I don't know when I've felt so good."

"Tommie," I replied, "I can't think of anything I'd rather do. I didn't know Christmas could be so much fun."

The New Year came in on a warm note, and I began to prepare for the first foals to be born in February. The four mares were all heavy now, but in blooming health. Roy and Tom took particular pride in them, and they often asked me if they could have this friend or that one come and see them. I always said yes.

Tommie laughed at our husband-like concern, and she asked me if I would be that attentive to her when she reached her eighth month. "Why, sure, honey," I replied. "I'll put new pine shavings in your bed, and feed you all the alfalfa you can eat."

She tossed a pillow at me in mock anger. She was even more light hearted than usual as her pregnancy advanced, in good health and glowing with happiness.

Way before daylight one morning in February I was awakened by the ringing of the phone: Roy said, "She's started," and hung up. I groped my way out of bed and into my clothes, being quiet so I wouldn't wake Tommie up, but she had heard the phone. "Is Beauty starting?" she asked.

"Yep, she is. You go on back to sleep, and I'll let you know when it's all over."

Tommie sat right up in bed. "Oh, no you don't, Joe Garth. You go on, and as soon as I can get dressed I'll be down there. I've never seen a foal born, and I wouldn't miss it for the world."

When I arrived at the large foaling box, Tom was seated on an overturned feed bucket looking through the fence, and Roy was inside the box leaning on one wall. The chestnut mare that we all called Beauty was lying on her side breathing rapidly. The tip of a tiny hoof could be seen at the opening of her vagina, and as she heaved another hoof and a nose appeared, and then slid back in as she relaxed. "Any problems, Roy?" I asked, as I slid through the gate.

"Not so far. The baby looks small, so I don't think she'll have any trouble." We spoke in quiet tones, for the mare was working hard and we didn't want to disturb her. She heaved again and the nose and second hoof appeared, pushed out further. Then Beauty began to flop up and down on the floor, throwing her head up and then her shoulder, and flopping back down with a jar. Each time she made this movement more of the foal appeared until the head and shoulders were out, with one leg clear and the other slightly bent back. Roy and I watched with blank faces knowing that this was not unusual. Some mares never moved, some stood up, and some flopped when they were foaling, some did all three, with variations.

Tommie had arrived and was leaning on the fence next to

Tom. "Won't that hurt her, Joe?" she asked.

Without taking my eyes off the horse, I replied, "No, it won't hurt her or the foal. Some mares flop like that to help the process along."

For several minutes Beauty strained and flopped, but the foal didn't move out any further. Roy said, "It looks like the left leg is hung up on her pelvic bone, Joe."

"I think you're right," I replied as I eased my way in behind the mare, talking to her quietly. When I reached the position I wanted, I squatted down, gently took hold of the foal's left leg at the fetlock, and spoke to Beauty. "Okay, girl. Go ahead and push, and I'll help you."

As if waiting for that suggestion, the mare grunted and pushed, I pulled on the leg, and out popped the baby. The foal, a fine stud colt, sneezed and began to move his head around as I moved back to the wall of the box. We wanted the horse to do everything in as natural a way as possible, even though some help had been necessary. Beauty lay on her side for just a bit, and then rolled over onto her chest. The baby horse was struggling, trying to stand, and not having much luck. His legs were too weak and shaky.

Now the mare heaved herself up onto her feet and shook all over, and then she turned around and nosed her new baby, murmuring to him in horse mama talk. I nodded to Roy, and we eased out of the box to stand beside Tom and Tommie and look at the new arrival.

"What a beautiful foal," Tommie said as she watched the mare begin to lick her baby. He was a deep sorrel color with a white diamond in the center of his forehead. His right front leg was white from the hoof to the knee, just like his mother. Of course, his color could change and it would be two or three years before anyone would know exactly what color he would be. Some foals retained their birth color, but most went through what horsemen called a "crazy quilt" period when they were covered by variations of all the colors in the line.

"Oh, yes," Roy replied. "He's going to be a winner."

I just smiled. This was the first of the long line of great horses I wanted to see born on the place. Some of the colts with lesser qualities would be gelded and sold for saddle stock, but this little guy had the look of a stallion already. If he turned out to be as good as he looked, I would hire a halter trainer and begin showing him at six months.

In quick succession over the next days the other mares foaled, all with no complications. Tommie and I were very proud of our little horse herd, and we often invited friends to come and see the new babies.

Easter was approaching, and Tommie had to have some new clothes. She was in her seventh month of pregnancy, so, of course, none of the dressy clothes she had would fit her. "Joe, I want to go buy some new clothes, and I'd like to do that in Dallas. Do you want to come along?"

I loved my wife very much, but taking her on a shopping trip to Dallas gave me the shudders. I didn't answer, but I gave her a painful look, and she laughed. "Oh, I know. You'd rather chase cows in a blizzard than go shopping in Big D. How about if I take Rita's daughter, Elena? She and I both like to shop, and she can drive."

"That would be fine, Tommie. Isn't Elena Madeline's mother?"

"Yes, she is. She works at Wal-Mart, so I don't get to see her as much as we'd both like, but we'll go on her day off, this Saturday. Do you want to baby-sit Madeline while we're gone?"

"Why, sure, if Madeline and Elena want me to. I'm going to take a ride over to the oil well site, and Madeline might like to see that."

When Elena came she brought a beaming five-year-old with her. As soon as Madeline was released from her car seat, she ran to me and jumped into my waiting arms "Uncle Joe! I'm going to baby-sit you! Isn't that great?"

The two women and I were all laughing at the exuberant little girl. "You bet it is, Maddie," I replied. "And we're going to have fun!" Elena gave me Madeline's safety seat, and she and

Tommie were ready to go.

We waved as Tommie and Elena backed the Expedition out of the garage and turned up the driveway, and then went back into the house. Rita came in from the kitchen and scooped her granddaughter up for a big hug. "Oh! What a big girl you are, Madeline Maria," she said as she bounced her up and down. "Hi, Grandma!" the little girl replied. "Do you have a lunch bag for us to take along on our trip?"

Rita laughed, and said, "Why, I didn't know you were going on a trip," but of course she did. The lunch bag was produced, and soon Madeline and I were traveling down U.S. Highway 287 toward Bowie. When we arrived at the well, I parked a good ways away and we watched as casing pipe was lowered into the hole. In a little while, Howard Reagan saw the pickup and came over to talk to us. He smiled at Madeline who had her hands over her ears to close out the screeching sound of the pipe, and said, "Joe, we're already drilling the next well. This one will be ready to pump before long and then you'll have some income. Do you want to go see the drilling rig at the new site?"

"Sure thing, Howard. I'll follow you. And Howard, any income I have coming I'd like to reinvest in future drilling."

"Fine, Joe. Of course, that will mean that you'll have a larger share in the company, and I'll be happy about that."

When I rolled up the window Madeline took her hands away from her ears and said, "That's a awful noise. My brothers say I make a awful noise when they tease me, but I'm not that loud."

I chuckled. "Well, get ready for more noise, Maddie. Drilling is worse than what you just heard."

The little girl pushed up the armrest between us, and snuggled up next to me. I hugged her, enjoying Madeline's company, and thinking that soon I would have a child of my own to hug. We bounced across rough pastureland until Howard's pickup stopped quite a ways from the drilling rig. The noise was loud and seemed to be getting louder as I got out of the pickup holding Maddie.

"There she is, Joe. We've named her the Reagan/Garth Number 2."

We watched for a while, but the noise was getting to Madeline, and I didn't like it much myself. We were leaning on the hood of the truck and Howard was behind us. I thought I heard the pickup door open, but when I turned to look it was closed and Reagan was leaning against it.

"Thanks for the tour, Howard," I finally said, and Maddie and I got in, I turned the truck around and headed back they way we'd come. My check book was on the dash in front of me, and I had a fleeting thought that its position had changed, but that thought was pushed aside when Maddie said, "I'm hungry, Uncle Joe."

We stopped at the park in Bowie to eat our sandwiches, and then went to McDonalds for ice cream. When we were done, I headed back to the ranch, and Madeline leaned back in her car seat to take a nap.

When we reached Highway 287, I turned toward home, but suddenly a loud explosion rolled over us like a visible presence. Looking back toward Bowie, I could see a great fireball hanging in the sky. I pulled over and we watched the fireball replaced by a long column of smoke. The position told me that it was very close to the finished well we had looked at not long before. I was tempted to turn and go back, but then I remembered Maddie was with me and decided not to. If it was our well, I'd hear soon enough.

Maddie hung on tight to me as we looked, and then she crawled back into her car seat and we drove on to the ranch. As soon as I stopped the pickup in front of the house, Rita came running out. "Oh, you're both all right," she exclaimed. "I thought you might have been caught in the oil well explosion." She quickly pulled Madeline out of her seat and hugged her hard.

"Did you see anything on the news, Rita?" I asked.

"Yes, and it's still on. A well belonging to the Reagan Drilling Company blew out. The report said two men were killed and several others injured."

In the den I was watching the news on TV when the phone rang. "Joe, this is Howard. I suppose you heard that Number One blew out."

"Just saw it on the news, Howard. Are you okay?"

"I'm fine. I was between the wells when it blew. Two of my men are dead, though, and three are badly injured. The fire is huge and we'll have to call in an oil fire team to put it out."

"Well, let's do it, Howard. I'm sure sorry to hear about your hands, though. Is there anything I can do?"

"Well, yes there is. I just called the Riley Control Company in Beaumont, and they'll come, but they have to have a down payment of $100,000.00. I'm pretty well overextended right now, so could you come up with that much today?"

I thought for a minute. "Yes, I can do that. Get the wiring instructions and I'll have my bank send it off."

"I've already got them. Got a pencil?" He read off the routing number and rang off.

I called Mr. Argus at the bank and gave him instructions along with the routing information. Argus agreed to wire the money, but he said, "Mr. Garth, when you have a minute we need to talk about your account."

I was suddenly alert. "What about my account, Mr. Argus?"

"Not over the phone, please Mr. Garth. Why don't you come in tomorrow morning and we'll chat?"

"All right. I'll be there about ten." I hung up and wondered what that too-slick banker was up to now.

CHAPTER TWENTY

Tommie and Elena returned while Madeline and I were down at the barns. Maddie was "helping" Roy feed the mares and foals, and I was inspecting the cattle while Tom poured feed for them in a long trough. The women came on down the winding path from the house dressed in their new finery, and seeing them coming, I let out a loud wolf-whistle.

At the whistle, the horses all raised their heads, and Maddie came running, her hands and face dirty: she'd been rubbing one of the foals behind the ears. "Mama!" she cried. "We saw a oil well, and the noise was awful!"

Tommie kissed me and Madeline and asked, "How did you do baby sitting Uncle Joe, Maddie?"

"Well," the little girl replied, holding tight to her mother's hand. "He didn't get into any trouble."

We all laughed, and Maddie smiled, knowing she was a hit.

I waited until we were alone to tell Tommie the bad news about the oil well. She said they had seen the column of smoke as they passed Bowie, so she knew there was a bad fire. "How much will it cost to put the blaze out, Joe?"

"I don't know for sure, but I wired one hundred thousand to the company in Beaumont that will be coming. I'm sure it will be more than that, but we'll just have to wait and see. Oh, yeah, when I talked to Argus at the bank, he said he wanted to see me about our account. I'm going in tomorrow morning to see what he's up to. Do you want to come along?"

Tommie smiled at me. "Joe, if you don't mind, I think I'll stay home tomorrow. Easter is close and I want to work on my outfit, with Rita's help."

"No problem, Tommie. Argus is not exactly a barrel of laughs anyway. I'll go in the morning and see what he wants."

What Winslow Argus wanted to talk about was how my account was shrinking. Even though there had been a substantial deposit after the cattle sale, the monthly draw for bill-paying was seriously depleting the original amount. Argus was all smiles and unction, but I still couldn't warm to the man. "So you see, Mr. Garth, if this keeps up you will soon find that your account is in serious trouble."

"Mr. Argus, believe it or not I already know about the account: I have a bookkeeper who sends me monthly statements.

True, I have spent a lot of money in the past year and a half, but I also have some sound investments that will begin to pay off in the next two to three years. Now, I have a question for you. What suggestions do you have to invest money at a higher rate of interest than your bank is paying me?"

Argus actually winced, and I could tell that he was not expecting that question. Argus had a problem that many professional people share; anyone outside their own realm of expertise is considered less intelligent. I had a hunch that he hadn't even consulted his own in-house investment broker because he wanted to keep my money working for his bank, but, of course, he couldn't say that. After all, as far as he was concerned, I was just an uneducated cowboy who didn't know that first thing about finance. "Well, Mr. Garth, there are only a limited number of investment products, and our bank always does the best it can to help our clients earn as much as possible. However, you have been spending your principal at an alarming rate, and we can't pay interest on money that has been spent. My suggestion would be that you stop spending your principal, and instead borrow from the bank when you need large sums of money. For instance, the $100,000.00 that you just wired to the oil fire fighting company. We could have loaned you that money at a reasonable rate, and you'd still have the money in your account."

I nodded. "Yes, and I'd be paying you more interest than you would be paying me."

"True, at least at the start. But when you paid off the loan, you would have the principal back. Doing it the way you did it means that one hundred thousand is gone forever."

I thought about this. The banker was right in thinking high finance was not my long suit, and I knew it. "Let me think about this for a while, Mr. Argus. I'll get back to you in a few days." I stood up, shook the bankers limp hand, and left.

From the bank I went to my accountant's office. Mr. Duckworth was in, and he was happy to see me. "Harold," I began, "I've just come from a visit to my banker, and he's given me some rather grim news about my account with him. You're my accountant, so maybe you can give me some financial advice. Argus tells me that if I keep on spending my principal, pretty soon it will all be gone. He suggested that I borrow money for large items and leave the principal to earn interest. What do you think?"

Duckworth was a very good CPA, and he never gave me any advice without knowing all of the facts. "May I call for your bookkeeper to bring in your books, Joe?"

We spent the next hour going over my financial bookwork. Finally, Harold said, "Joe, you *have* spent a lot of money, but you've also made some good investments. By my figures, if you had to liquidate today, you'd still have over three million dollars. Now, the problem is cash flow. You've already sent $100,000.00 to the Riley Control Company, do you anticipate having to spend more to get the oil fire under control?"

"I don't really know, but I think I will. Reagan doesn't have much cash, and it's bound to be an expensive operation."

"In that case, you would be wise to find out just how much you will be spending. There is a point where you might need to cut your losses and get out. You can certainly take the expense as a tax loss, but the money's still gone. How much are you willing to spend on this fire?"

I thought for a minute. "Well, I originally invested $500,000.00 with Reagan, and now I've added a further $100,000.00. I guess I'd go another hundred and that's it."

Duckworth used those figures to show me how much my tax savings would be if I took a total loss of $700,000.00. Finally, with a lot to think about, I thanked the CPA and left the office. Duckworth had cautioned me about borrowing heavily at the bank for risky investments, which to the accountant meant almost everything, and certainly included oil wells.

Back home with Tommie, I gave her a rundown on the financial situation, but she only smiled and hugged me. "Joe, having money's nice, but I don't really care if we're rich or poor. Let's enjoy the things we have, and if we have to give them up, we'll still make out."

I laughed and hugged her back. "You know, Tommie, I've still got Buck and my old pickup and trailer. That's what I started out with, and I reckon as long as I have those things for security, and you in my corner, nothing can really faze me."

"Didn't I hear Roy say he had a friend who wanted to buy your old pickup?"

"Yes, but I told him it wasn't for sale. I kind of like knowing it's still there if I ever need it."

Early the next morning Howard Reagan called again. "Joe, I've got bad news. Reagan/Garth #2 is a duster, and Riley is getting ready to start on the fire, but he says he needs more money. Can you come up with another hundred thousand?"

With my conversation with Duckworth still warm in my mind, I said, "Howard, I'll put in a hundred more, and that's it. Right now you're into me for $600,000.00 and no income in sight, so after this next hundred I'm cutting my losses. And, I want this extra two hundred thousand to add to the 500 that I paid at first. That means that my interest in your company is going to increase. Get the papers drawn up and bring them by."

It was quiet on the other end of the phone line, and then Reagan replied, "I can't say that I blame you, Joe, but unless we get this fire under control, there won't ever be anything from this well. If you'll wire the money today, I'll tell Riley it's coming and he can go ahead, and I'll have the paperwork to you tomorrow."

We disconnected, but neither of us was happy with the conversation.

CHAPTER
TWENTY-ONE

I was surprised one morning when Tommie announced that I needed to have a new suit made for Easter. She very rarely insisted on anything that had to do with my wardrobe, and I usually wore simple cow country clothes, though I did have some nice shirts and jeans that I would put on for special occasions, plus a pair of black ostrich skin boots. "But, I already have a suit," I said. "I bought one for our wedding, and I haven't worn it since. Why can't I just wear that one?"

We were sitting on the love seat in the den having coffee, and Tommie turned her most appealing look on her me, and I suppose like all wives, she really knew how to look appealing when she wanted something. "Joe, I want you to have a suit made to measure, like you have your boots made. There's a tailor in Las Colinas that I've heard is great. He makes suits for the Dallas Cowboys and other celebrities. Let's go see him and have him make you a suit."

I was shaking my head the moment Tommie mentioned Las Colinas. I hated the noise, the smells and the traffic in the Dallas/Fort Worth Metroplex, and I never went there if I could avoid it. And Las Colinas was right smack in the middle of the worst part. "No, Tommie, I'm not going to Dallas. If you think I need a suit, let's just go to the mall and I'll pick one up."

"Joe, please indulge me in this. You look really good in a suit, but in a tailored suit you'll look even better. I'll tell you what, if you don't want to go to Las Colinas, let's find a tailor in Wichita Falls and go there."

I thought I saw just a bit of deception in Tommie's quick switch from Las Colinas to Wichita Falls, but how could I deny her anything? "Okay, babe. Find one in Wichita and I'll go."

Tommie clapped her hands together. "I was hoping you'd say that!" she exclaimed. She turned to the lamp stand beside her and picked up a slip of paper. "I've already found one, and here's the address."

I snatched the paper from her, looked at it and tossed it back. Tommie was laughing hard now. "You little minx!" I shouted in mock anger. "You had this whole thing planned. You knew I'd settle for Wichita if I didn't have to go to the Metroplex!" I reached for her, but she jumped up and ran into the kitchen, her bubbling laughter following. I caught her there and tickled her until her eyes watered and we both fell down on the floor with the giggles.

Rita came out of her apartment to see what the noise was all about, and when I told her, she laughed along with us. Of course, I was sure Tommie had already told her what she planned to do when I caught the two women exchanging a conspiratorial wink.

The trip to the tailor was not nearly as bad as I anticipated. With Tommie's help I picked out a piece of dark blue wool with a faint black pinstripe, and the tailor measured me and said he'd have the suit ready for a first fitting in five days.

On Easter morning Tommie and I arrived at the Chapel of Peace several minutes before the service started, both wearing our new finery. The church was packed, but one of Rita's granddaughters – Angelina – had been stationed in the vestibule to watch for us, and she quickly led us through the crowd to two seats saved and waiting. Before we could sit down, Madeline appeared and hugged my leg, and then she held up her arms for me to pick her up, which I did with a large smile on my face.

The service was great, with much singing and special music, and we enjoyed every minute of it. When it was over, we invited Rita's entire family to go to a restaurant with us for Easter lunch, but Rita had made other plans. "No," she said, "not today. You are coming with us to Elena's house for Easter dinner."

And some dinner it was, far better than anything a restaurant could serve. Tommie and I left in mid-afternoon, filled with good food and friendship. "What a great family Rita has," Tommie said as we headed home. I just nodded and patted my stomach.

CHAPTER TWENTY-TWO

By the time we reached home, I was ready for a nap, and after I changed clothes I dropped gratefully into my recliner to let the rich food I'd eaten settle. I was dreaming of cattle grazing in knee-deep grass when I was jerked awake by a loud cry. For just a minute I stayed in the chair with my eyes open, wondering if I'd really heard anything, and then Tommie cried, "Joe! Joe!"

I rushed to the bedroom where Tommie had gone to lie down, and found her writhing in pain. "Joe! The baby's coming!"" she gasped.

I quickly picked her up and rushed out to the Expedition we had left in the driveway. By the time I reached the highway and headed into town, Tommie was moaning with pain and bleeding heavily. I kept my foot down and when I hit the freeway leading into town a police car pulled up beside me with lights flashing. I pointed in the direction of the hospital and didn't slow down. The policeman got the message and pulled in front of me to clear traffic and serve as an escort. With the policeman's help, we were soon pulling into the covered emergency entrance of the Wichita Falls General Hospital.

I pulled to a fast stop and leaped out of the car calling in a loud voice, "Bring a stretcher!" The policeman went through the doors ahead of me, and as I carried my unconscious wife through the entrance, two men met me pushing a gurney. They quickly took Tommie out of my arms, laid her on the cart, and wheeled her on into the hospital calling out, *"Move! We've got a bleeder!"*

As they pushed the gurney through the doors of an operating room, I was stopped by a kindly nurse. "Please let us do our jobs, sir. You stay out here, and we'll let you know what's happening as soon as possible."

I stopped, my heart beating fast, but with nothing else to do I walked over to a chair and sat down. I felt dazed, confused and badly frightened. Tommie! Surely she'd be all right. I looked up at the ceiling and prayed, "Oh, God. Please take care of her! Please!"

The policeman who had led me in came into the waiting room and said, "Sir, I don't mean to intrude, but you really should move your car while you have a chance. It's right in the middle of the bay where the ambulances pull in."

I shook my head trying to make sense of what the officer was saying. The words finally got through, and I nodded and stood up. "Are you the one who led me into town?" I asked.

"Yes, sir," The policeman replied.

"Thanks, officer. That was a big help." I reached out to shake the man's hand.

Together we walked through the doors and over to my car, and the officer said, "I hope your wife will be all right," and continued on to his own car.

"Thanks," I mumbled. I climbed behind the wheel and, bowing my head, I prayed again, "Oh, God, please, *please* let her be all right."

Somehow time passed. I sat or stood as near the room where they had taken Tommie as I could get, and finally, a doctor emerged from the room wearing green scrubs, with a white mask dangling under his chin. "Mr. Garth?" he asked.

"Is she going to be all right?"

The doctor didn't reply, just slowly shook his head.

"You mean she's not going to be all right? Can I see her?"

"Mr. Garth, I'm sorry. We did all we could but we couldn't stop the bleeding. I'm afraid your wife didn't make it." The doctor placed a hand on my shoulder and squeezed.

"No!" I cried. "She can't be dead!" and I dropped into the chair behind me as if my legs would no longer hold me up and buried my face in my hands.

"Mr. Garth, we did save the baby. She's healthy and she's near enough to full term that I think she'll do fine. She's in an incubator right now, but I imagine that will only be for today."

I heard him speak, but the words didn't register. Tommie, Tommie. What am I going to do without Tommie? Who would share my dreams? How can I go on? *"I'm not going anywhere that you won't be able to find me, Joe. You couldn't lose me if you wanted to."* But how could I find her now?

I sat on in the chair, my mind a whirl. What now? I didn't know. The hospital became busy, with people moving by, sometimes at a run, but I didn't really pay any attention. Finally the kindly nurse who had spoken to me earlier came to tell me I could see my new daughter. I looked at her with a mind totally unfocused. "What did you say?" I asked.

"I said you may now see your brand new daughter, Mr. Garth."

"A baby? You mean Tommie's baby is alive?"

"Yes, sir. I'm real sorry about your wife, but at least we saved the baby."

I stood and slowly followed the nurse like a robot. She took me to a dressing room, fitted me with a sterile gown, mask and gloves, and then opened the door into the nursery. There, in a side room stood a row of incubators, and she stopped at the first one. I looked into the glass window on the top and saw a tiny baby girl, lying on her back with her eyes closed.

"You can put your hands through here and touch her if you want. She has just been fed and she probably won't wake up." The nurse showed me the opening where I could insert my gloved hands. With wonder, I touched baby's tiny shoulder, rubbing my finger gently back and forth and watched her chest move up and down as she breathed. In spite of my shock and sadness, I felt a small smile pulled at the corners of my mouth.

After a few minutes, I pulled my hands back out and looked at the nurse. "Tommie was sure we would have a girl, I don't know how. Neither of us wanted a sonogram to prove the baby's sex, but she just knew we would have a girl. And we talked names, so I have a name for her: Ashley Lillian Garth."

"Fine, Mr. Garth. The doctor will put that on her birth certificate. You can come see her anytime you want, you know."

"Thanks, Ami, I'll do that."

I left the nursery and walked in a daze out to the car. There I sat for some time trying to think of what I should do next, and then it hit me, I had to call Tommie's folks and tell them. I picked up the phone and made the hardest call of my life. Before it ended, all three of us were in tears.

CHAPTER TWENTY-THREE

The next days went by in a fog-bound haze for me. I seemed to be in a dark mental room that I couldn't find my out of. Between them, Fred, Lillian and Rita took care of funeral details and other things, with me signing my name on any document they presented. I made only one request, and since it was also Tommie's, there was no hesitation on the part of her folks or Rita. She was to be buried in a private graveside ceremony with a closed casket. Only the family and close friends would be invited. Handy and Matt came in from the Slash T, sorry for my loss, and grieving with me. The crew from the ranch came, and all of Rita's family. Little Madeline hugged me and said, "Uncle Joe, I'm so sorry about Aunt Tommie. I pray for her and you." I hugged the little girl tight and the tears slid down my cheeks.

When the graveside service was over, I wiped my eyes and hugged Lillian and Fred. Roy and the other hands and Rita's family all tried to touch me or say something, and I nodded, but I didn't really hear them. Finally, I slowly made my way over to the pickup and drove away.

Pastor Whiting had been a comfort to me after Tommie's death, sitting with me quietly for hours at a time, and I know he followed me with his eyes as I left the cemetery. I thought about our prayer together before the funeral. "Lord, we have no idea why things happen the way they do, but we do know that you are always with us. Now, Joe needs to feel your presence more than ever. Do you have someone in mind to help him bear this loss? Oh, I see that you have provided that someone already. Thank you. Amen." And I thought of the tiny girl in the hospital nursery and realized what the pastor meant.

Every day I went to the hospital as if drawn by a magnate. Ashley was moved out of the incubator on the second day, and I could hold her, such a tiny bundle, my only link to Tommie. I spent every moment I could with the little girl in my arms I learned to feed her and change her and croon her to sleep. She was so tiny that at first I was afraid I might injure her in some way, but the nurses assured me that she needed to be held and cuddled by her daddy, and I soon lost my fear and treasured the time spent at the hospital. I told Tommie all about our baby, feeling her presence with us, as if she were looking over my shoulder.

Fred and Lillian came every day too, and they also held their granddaughter some, but they often just sat and watched me hold her. I knew they were grieving for their daughter, too, but at least they had each other to lean on. If I thought about things at all, I knew I would probably go out of my mind if it were not for Ashley. I had loved Tommie so much that my grief would have been unbearable.

One morning when I was sitting in the private room I had arranged feeding Ashley, a doctor came in and surprised me by saying, "Mr. Garth, if Ashley continues to do as well as she has been doing, you can take her home next week."

Up to that point I hadn't really thought about how I would care for the baby once she left the hospital. I knew I would have to have help, and I couldn't just expect Rita to take over. "Well, Doc, I'll need some help. Do you know anyone I can hire as a nanny?"

"No, but I'll ask the head nurse. I'm sure she'll have a list and a recommendation."

The nurse came up to me as I was leaving and gave me a list with three names on it. "Any one of these three will be fine. The first two are LVN's with hospital experience. The third is a retired social worker that lives alone. You might want to try her first."

"Thank you," I said. "You and all the nurses have been very kind to me and Ashley. I reckon there's no way I can tell you how much I appreciate it."

She smiled at me, a sad smile, and I went on out to my pickup.

On my way back to the ranch that day I stopped in front of a modest home on Collins Avenue where Wendy Seth, the retired social worker lived. My knock was answered by a vigorous woman in her mid-sixties. She was short and thin, with kind brown eyes and graying black hair. She invited me to come in, and the interview with her went well. I liked her warmth and

169

common sense, and I hired her on the spot. "I'll be by tomorrow to pick you up, Wendy," I said, as she didn't own a car, and she agreed.

When I arrived the next day she smiled and said, "I'm all ready, Mr. Garth."

I picked up her two bags and put them in the back seat of the truck, and then helped her into the passenger seat. Soon we were at the ranch, and I introduced Wendy to Rita. "Please show Wendy to her room, Rita, and help her get settled. I'm going to pick up the Mannings and go get Ashley." I left as the two ladies were getting acquainted.

When we arrived at the hospital, I pushed Lillian's wheel-chair into the elevator and then out at the third floor where the nursery was located. When the nurse handed the baby to me, I gently laid her in Lillian's arms, and both grandparents began to cry. "Let's go, folks," I said in a low voice, and pushed Lillian's chair back the way we had come.

In the car, I drove and Fred and Lillian sat in the back seat passing the baby back and forth, and making comments: "She's got your eyes, Lil." "Fred, I think her hair's going to be curly on top just like Tommie's." Ashley's eyes were as blue as the sky, and what little hair she had was a fine blond fuzz on top of her head.

At the ranch Lillian held the baby once again while Fred pushed her into the house with me holding the doors open. Wendy was waiting, and after introductions she took Ashley to the nursery to change her.

"Joe," Fred said. "Lillian and I want you to know that we will help you with Ashley in any way we can. Just call us at any time, day or night, and we'll be here."

"Thanks, Fred. You'll be the first ones I call. And don't think I don't know how much you've already done. I couldn't have gotten through the ---," I couldn't say funeral, "those days without you."

Later, I asked Wendy and Rita to come into the den where

I was feeding Ashley. "You two ladies are now in charge of the household. Rita, you know your duties, and they haven't changed. You will be next to me in decision making, and Wendy, you will be in charge of everything to do with Ashley, under my direction. Rita will help you get settled in.

"Now, Wendy, I do not expect to be an absent father. I hired you because I need help, but whenever possible, I will be taking care of Ashley. I *want* to take care of her in all ways possible. However, I want you to do anything that needs to be done when I'm not around. For instance, I will get up in the night to feed the baby, but if I'm gone over night, that will be your job. If I'm inside and she needs to be fed or changed, either of us can handle that, but I prefer to do it as often as possible. Does this make sense to you?"

"Well, yes it does, Mr. Garth. You want me to be here to take care of Ashley when needed, but you don't want me to be a surrogate mother. Is that right?"

I beamed at her. "I knew from our first meeting that you were smart, and now you've proven it. That is *just* what I want. Now then, Rita has her paycheck deposited into her bank account, do you want me to have the bookkeeper do the same with yours?"

"Yes, sir, I do. And I want to say that you can depend on me to be just what you want in a nanny."

"Thank you, Wendy. And Rita, you know how much I appreciate you. With you two ladies helping me, I don't think we can go far wrong.

"Now, one other thing. I'm going to buy you a car so that one or both of you can go to town if the need arises. Rita, I believe you told me that you don't have a license, how about you, Wendy?"

"Yes sir, I do have a license. I had an old car, but it just got too expensive to keep, so I sold it last year."

"Fine. You pick out a new car of whatever brand you like, and I'll buy it for you. That way, if I'm gone and you need to get something for yourselves or the baby, you can go ahead and get it. And I don't mean you just have to use it for baby or ranch business. The car will belong to you two ladies to use any way you want.

"Now, I don't want any hurt feelings, so Rita, you tell me how this idea sets with you."

Rita smiled in her quiet way. "I think its fine, Joe. Wendy and I will have no problems at all, and having a car will help out."

That night I sat by Ashley's little bed, looking at the tiny form lying there. She was sleeping peacefully, lying on her back, eyes closed, breathing easily. Gently I laid a finger on her palm, and her little fist curled around it. "Oh, Tommie, Tommie," I whispered. "She's everything we wanted, why can't you be here with us?" Tears slid down my cheeks as I bowed my head and prayed. "I just don't understand, God. She was so good, so good..."

After while I chuckled and said, "Tommie, I was feeding Ashley tonight, and I put her up on my shoulder to burp her like the nurses taught me. She promptly spit curdled milk all over my shirt. And when I pulled her back down, she immediately dirtied her diaper, as if to say, 'Get to work, Daddy.' Oh, Tommie. How I wish you were here......."

CHAPTER TWENTY-FOUR

As the weeks rolled by, I slowly moved back into the work around the ranch, but I was with Ashley every possible minute. She was only six months old when I first sat her on a horse.

Of course, she didn't really know what was happening, but she trusted me, and the picture Rita took showed a huge smile on her face. After that, on nice days I would often take her with me when I rode the pastures, and soon she was looking forward to our rides.

Things might have appeared to be back to normal on the surface, but I knew that I was a changed man. I was no longer the carefree cowboy that had won the lottery. I seemed to only smile when I was around Ashley, and I never felt like laughing anymore. The pain of the loss was still very real, and I was sure all of my friends wondered if I would ever recover from Tommie's death. I wondered the same thing.

Fred and Lillian came to the ranch often to see Ashley, and I took her to visit them at least once a week so that Ashley would know her grandparents. But when they or anyone else tried to talk about Tommie, I left the room. I knew I was often hurting them, but I was not ready to talk about her. My wounds were slowly healing, and I didn't want them to reopen.

Easter was very difficult for me, and on Ashley's first birthday I had a hard time keeping my emotions under control. Rita and Wendy arranged a birthday party for the little girl, inviting her grandparents, the ranch workers, and Rita's family. Little Madeline, now almost six, still stayed close to me, her favorite "uncle," and she thought tiny Ashley was the nearest thing to a living doll she had ever seen.

The party was a success, but I was glad when it was over. I wanted my daughter to always enjoy her birthday and not associate it with the pain I remembered, and I was determined that she should not see me looking sad.

The next year went by fast, and Ashley grew into a sweet natured little girl, even though she was doted on by me and her grandparents, and catered to by both Rita and Wendy. Her second birthday party was more fun for her and all involved, and it was easier for me; though the pain was still there, time alone had eased it.

The party was on Thursday evening, and the house was

still decorated on Friday morning when Harold Duckworth called. "Joe, did you authorize more money for the burned out oil well that Reagan is trying to recover?"

"Why, no, Harold. I don't think I did. But you know I haven't been paying much attention to the oil business the last couple of years, and I haven't talked to Howard for quite a while."

"Well, I think we need to meet. You can come in here, or I'll go out there. Which suits you better?"

"I'll come in this morning, Harold."

"Okay. See you in a bit."

When I had a cup of coffee at my elbow, Duckworth showed me a cancelled check with my signature on it. The check was for $250,000.00. "Did you write this check, Joe?" he asked.

I looked at the signature. It was very close to mine, but the "t" in Garth was crossed with an up slant, rather than my own down slant. "No, I didn't. I've been in a fog and I know I haven't paid much attention to business matters since... but I didn't write this check. The signature is forged, and it's dated two weeks ago. My bookkeeper writes all the normal business and household checks, but her authority doesn't apply to something this large."

"That's what I thought," Harold said. "I matched it against other signatures on cancelled checks here in the office, and it didn't look exactly right. It appears that Howard Reagan forged a check on your account."

Now, when a phone call from my banker would have helped, Argus kept quiet and cashed the check. It was time to change banks. I sat in thought for a minute, and then said, "Let's call him up and ask him."

Harold handed me the phone. It rang several times, and then I heard Reagan's voice with a background of oil well noise. "Hello."

"Howard, it's Joe Garth. I'm sitting in my accountant's

office looking at a cancelled check for $250,000.00 made out to you with a phony signature. Know anything about it, Howard?"

The line was still open, but Reagan wasn't speaking. "I take it from your silence that you *do* know something about it. Now, you drop what you're doing and get yourself in here. I'll give you thirty minutes before I call the police. The address is 506 West Kemp." Before Reagan could answer, I hung up the phone.

In less than half an hour, a red-faced Howard Reagan in oil-spattered clothes entered Duckworth's office. "Joe, I can explain," he said immediately.

I was still seated. I had not stood in politeness as I would normally have done, and I looked up at the oilman and replied, "It'll take a lot explaining to come up with a good reason to steal a quarter of a million dollars, Reagan, but let's hear it."

"Well, you know when your wife died, I was just starting to overhaul the well, and the money just seemed to drain away. The last two years have been a real struggle. I've tried everything, but I just couldn't come up with any money. I know you're still not over your wife's death, so I didn't want to bother you again. I knew if it had been any other time, I could have asked you and you would have okayed the check, so I just went ahead and wrote it out and cashed it."

"And just how did you get one of my checks, Reagan?"

Now the man's head dropped in at least mock embarrassment. "The last time you were out at the lease your checkbook was on the dashboard of your truck. While you were looking at the well, I just sort of borrowed the last check in the book, just in case of emergencies, Joe! You know I'd never steal from you. I just needed money to get that well producing again, and it seemed the only way at the time. I didn't want to bother you in your grief, and I knew you'd understand."

Up to this point Duckworth had made no comment. He was amazed, but not really surprised, at Reagan's comments and his justification of what could only be called a criminal act. Now he said, "Do you have enough money to make this check good, Mr. Reagan?"

Reagan shook his head. "No, I don't. Everything I have is tied up in that well and the equipment I need to bring it back on line."

I looked at the man before me, perhaps really seeing him for the first time. We were not friends, though we had been friendly business partners, evidently *too* friendly on my part. Reagan had taken advantage of my grief and openhandedness, and while I might forgive the latter, I would never forgive the former. "In thirty days from today, Howard Reagan, you will meet me here in Mr. Duckworth's office with a bankers check for $950,000.00, my original investment plus the money I advanced for the fire fighters, and this money you stole. If you do not have the money here, I will prosecute you for forging my name on this check. Because of the amount involved, I think that will mean prison time for you. At least, I will do everything in my power to bring that about."

I stood and walked up to the shocked oilman. "Now," I said in a low, dangerous voice, "get out of my sight before I forget myself and rearrange your face!"

Both Reagan and Duckworth were shocked by my hard, vicious voice. Neither of them had ever seen me display anger of any kind. I had always been pretty mild mannered and happy-go-lucky, but no more. Reagan had touched the most hurtful point in my life, and I meant every word I said. Almost stumbling in haste, Howard Reagan wheeled and left the office. "Will you prosecute, Joe?" Duckworth asked.

I waited to answer until I recovered from my anger. "Yes, I will, Harold. I can forgive a lot, even the theft of a quarter of a million dollars, but I can't forgive a man who took advantage of my grief to line his own pockets." I asked the accountant to get my lawyer on the phone, and we started the ball rolling for a suit against Reagan. My attorney, Jacob Newalter, would also write up a report for the police in case the oilman didn't pay up in 30 days. We charged him with grand theft and forgery.

When I returned home, Ashley wanted to go for a ride, so the two of us went down to the barn and saddled up Buck and Ashley's new pony; she had named him Star. It was not hard to put the problems with the oilman behind me, and soon I was smiling and calling out encouragement as the little girl rode her slow horse around the sales arena. She was fearless and wanted to go out into the big pasture, but I told her that would have to wait. Buck was resigned to following the pony around the arena, though he also would rather be loping across the pastures.

We finished our ride just at lunchtime, and after taking care of the horses, we went back up to the house. Rita had a meal all ready, and she and Wendy ate with us. While we were eating I said, "Ashley, how would you like to take a little trip with me? There are some cattle I want to look at down around Bandera, and we could stay down there for a few days."

"Yes!" Ashley shouted. She had no idea where Bandera was, but she loved to go places, and wherever I went she wanted to go.

Rita and Wendy both gave me a look that said, *"Can we talk about this?"* and I grinned at them and nodded.

Later, when Ashley was taking a nap, the ladies tried to talk me out of taking her with me. "She's too little to go on such a long trip," Wendy said. And Rita chimed in with, "Joe, are you sure you want to take her? She may be a lot of trouble for you."

I laughed, and I realized it was the first time I had really laughed since the funeral. "You two mother hens will just have to get by without your chick for a few days. I know she's young, and I know I'll have to take care of her, but Ashley's going to make a lot of trips with me, and I want her to start now. We'll leave tomorrow and be gone for five days, but I'll call you two every day and give you a 'chick report.'"

Neither of them was very happy with my answer to their fears, but they both knew that when my mind was made up, there was no changing it, so they stopped trying.

The next morning we left at eight o'clock, and the two

mother hens waved from the front porch, still not happy about seeing their beloved little girl going off on a long trip without them.

We took it easy going south. Ashley was confined to her car seat, and while it was comfortable enough, she often wanted out. We also had to make frequent potty stops and food stops. When we reached Kerrville it was late afternoon, and I pulled into the Sunday House Inn where we would stay for a few days.

Since Ashley had never slept anywhere but in her own bed, she was uncomfortable in the second big bed in the motel suite. After fussing for thirty minutes, I finally gave up and put her in bed with me. That was all it took, and she soon snuggled down next to me and was sleeping peacefully.

Looking down at the little girl, a real carbon copy of her mother, except her hair was blond, I felt a great sadness. Tommie should be with us, and we should both be enjoying this child we had longed for. I lay awake far into the night in grief over what might have been.

The next morning we had a light breakfast at the motel, and then drove the twenty-six miles south to Bandera, a quiet ranching town set in the Texas Hill Country, and on to the H Bar H Ranch a few miles further south.

The cattle that I wanted to see were all young registered Angus cows, with calves at side and bred back. When we arrived at the ranch, the owner came out to meet us, along with his wife. Mrs. McFarland was surprised to see that I had my two-year-old daughter with me, and she immediately volunteered to take care of Ashley while Mr. McFarland I looked at the cattle, but I smiled and gently refused. "Ashley's going to own a ranch someday, so she might as well learn about cattle early." Mrs. McFarland understood, and she came with us when we went to see the young cows.

The cattle were in fine shape, and I liked them. Bob McFarland and I began to talk price, haggling back and forth for a while. The McFarland's asked us to stay for lunch, and I accepted. The food was good, and while McFarland and I talked some more about price, nothing had been settled by the time I took a sleepy Ashley back to the motel. We did agree to talk again the next day, however.

After Ashley's nap and my promised call to Rita and Wendy, we went down to the pool. There was a nice shallow wading pool next to the large one, and I sat back with a book while Ashley splashed and played with a floating dragon brought along for the purpose.

When we entered our room at 4:30, the phone was ringing. "Hello," I said. I had a cell phone, but mostly I left it in the truck turned off.

"Joe, this is Harold Duckworth. I've been trying to reach you all day. I just learned from a lawyer friend that Howard Reagan is being sued, and you're named as his partner."

"What does that mean?" I asked.

"It means that whatever the judgment is for, if the other side wins, you will be liable for a percentage of Reagan's debts."

"Wait a minute! That man stole $250,000.00 from me, and I'll be liable for *his* debts? Surely you're wrong."

"I'm afraid not, Joe. I'll contact Jacob and give him a heads up if you wish."

"Please do that, Harold, and I'll call you as soon as I get back sometime tomorrow."

When I hung up, I thought for a minute, and then called Bob McFarland to tell him something had come up and we would have to return home, but I'd be in touch. Then I looked down at Ashley and noticed her worried look. "What's wrong, baby?" I asked.

"You look sad, Daddy. Are you hurt?" In the little girl's small fund of experience, only a "hurt" would make anyone sad.

I reached down, picked my daughter up and gave her a big kiss. "No, Ashley, I'm not hurt. Let's go have something to eat. Where do you want to go?"

She smiled all over her face and replied, "MacDonuls!" her favorite place no matter where we were.

As I sat on a bench in the play area at McDonalds watching

Ashley play on the slide, I began to put things in perspective. Here was the most important thing in my life, this little girl. Far more important than money, or oil wells, or crooked drillers, or lawyers, or even buying more cattle. As long as I had Ashley with me, none of that other stuff really mattered.

We both slept well that night; me unbothered by what might be happening in Wichita Falls, and Ashley in her own bed *"like a big girl."*

The drive home next day was leisurely. We stopped often and got out to play and run around. I called Harold, who had no further news, to say we would be in late and I would phone him the next day.

At 10:00 p.m. I laid a sleepy little girl down in her own bed, watched by Rita and Wendy. The women left the room, but I stayed on, sitting by her bed, one of her tiny hands wrapped around my finger. In a drowsy voice she said, "We had fun didn't we Daddy?"

"Yes, baby," I whispered. "We had fun." And I watched as the little girl breathed her way to sleep land.

CHAPTER
TWENTY-FIVE

Jacob Newalter was a short, round man in a rumpled suit. His little remaining hair was long at the sides, curling down over his ears. He didn't look like the typical lawyer, whatever that was, but he welcomed me into his office, and we began to talk about the case. Newalter suggested that we notify the police and charge Howard Reagan with forgery and theft, and then file the suit, and I agreed. "Mr. Garth," Jacob said, "I've got to tell you that the opposition has a very good case. Reagan is truly stretched thin, and he has no real assets. Most of his drilling equipment is leased, and what oil wells he's getting royalties from are all attached. Since you have some money, I have a feeling that no plaintiff will want to dismiss your position."

"Who's suing Reagan, Jacob?"

"A group of his creditors got together and hired a big firm out of Dallas to represent them. Evidently Reagan owes money all over Texas, Oklahoma and Louisiana. There are nineteen plaintiffs listed in the suit."

I left Newalter's office feeling like a man painted into a corner. When I arrived home it was with a sense of great relief. I had lunch with Ashley and Wendy, and then went down to the barns. Roy met me there and we went to look at the horses. Handy's Own was on a low protein diet now that his mares were all in foal again, and he came to the fence and nickered when he saw me. "I think I'll saddle him up and take a ride, Roy," I said.

Roy snapped a lead rope around the stallion's neck and led him to the tack room. When I had the saddle cinched up, I led the horse out to a gate into the south pastures, mounted, and was soon loping over the rolling countryside. With a sense of real freedom, I shrugged off the worries about lawsuits and Howard Reagan, and just enjoyed the ride.

The next days went by slowly. I spent as much time as possible with Ashley and my livestock, and I found myself getting back to what really interested me – working with cattle and horses, and teaching my daughter about the animals. I didn't call my lawyer, and I didn't really care what happened in the lawsuit. I decided to adopt a cowboy outlook: whatever happened would just have to happen. In the mean time, I planned to enjoy myself.

Sunday morning, and I arrived at church carrying Ashley.

I sat her down as I saw Rita and her clan bearing down us. Ashley was dressed in a new outfit, a pale yellow dress with a full skirt and a stiff-starched ruffle. I'd brushed her fine blond hair until it shined, and she was smiling like an angel. Rita had helped me buy the dress, and she had ironed it herself.

Sitting in a row of chairs, surrounded by Rita's family, I felt right at home. Ashley was sitting on my lap, and Madeline was right next to me, hugging my arm. The service started with lively music, and I relaxed, knowing that I was in the right place at the right time.

Of course, nothing would do but that Ashley and I go to Elena's for Sunday dinner, and we all laughed and had a lot of fun. Rita had been teaching Ashley Spanish, and she could rattle on in two languages like the other kids. By the time we left to go home, Ashley had had so much fun she was drooping with sleep, and in fact, when we reached the house, she didn't even open an eye as I removed her pretty dress and tucked her into bed.

I was reading the paper in the den when the phone rang. "Joe," Jacob Newalter said, "sorry to disturb you on Sunday, but I've just learned from a friend that your assets will be frozen by court order tomorrow morning. The lawyers for the conglomerate want to make sure that you don't send your money somewhere that they can't reach."

"Does that mean their going to try to get all the money Reagan owes them out of me?" I asked.

"Well, you're only liable for the percentage of his business you own, but I'm afraid they'll probably make the judgment expenses and punitive damages as high as they can. Then, if they win the suit, the judge will actually set the amount owed by you and Reagan. Of course, since he doesn't have any money, you will be the one who will actually pay. Doesn't seem fair, does it Mr. Garth?"

I laughed, for some reason nearly unfazed by the threat of losing all my money. "Now, Jacob, I've been around for a long time, and I've found that life is life, and fairness rarely comes into it. Do you have any suggestions for me?"

"I can't legally tell you to hide your money, Joe. I can't tell you to transfer the deed to your ranch to your daughter, or to put most of your money in a trust fund for her. Do you understand that I can't tell you to do these things?"

"I understand, Jacob, but I'll not follow those ideas that you can't tell me about for two very good reasons. One is that I already have an unbreakable trust established for Ashley, and two is that I won't run and hide. If you will estimate your fee for the next few weeks, I will get you some money early tomorrow before the accounts are frozen. I'll also go to the bank and get enough cash to take care of expenses for a month. Then it's up to you."

"Joe, I respect your integrity, even if I don't agree with your logic," Jacob replied.

Later in the evening Miles Moore called to tell me how sorry he was about recommending Reagan. "I'd give anything if I hadn't made that call, Joe. I hope you'll forgive me."

"Nothing to forgive, Miles. Even though you introduced us, I made the decision to trust the man. Anyway, don't worry about it. Somehow this whole money thing has seemed like a dream to me, sometimes a good one, sometimes not so good. If I get out of this mess, I think I'll sell up, put the money that's left, if any, in a trust, and go back to being a cowboy. If I put the ranch on the market, would you like the listing?"

"Joe, you are the most forgiving man I know. Not only would I like the listing, you won't believe how low my commission will be."

We traded a few more pleasantries, and rang off.

The next morning early I took a check by for the lawyer, cashed another check for money to see me through the next weeks, and transferred ownership of the car Rita and Wendy used to them as joint owners. At least that much I would do before my assets were frozen,

The next days and weeks went by in a whirl of court appearances and official documents. Through it all, however, I felt amazingly calm. I rode around the ranch with Ashley, and worked cows with Roy and Tom. I even went to local cattle sales, though not to buy. I called Mr. MacFarland at Bandera and told him I would not be buying any more cattle. I was sorry about that, but I would sure tell other people how good the MacFarland Black Angus cattle were.

I did move a few things from the ranch, but not in the sneaky way my lawyer had *not* suggested. I hitched the beat up trailer to my old Ford pickup, loaded Buck and Star, Ashley's pony, along with their tack, and drove around to Fred and Lillian's ranch. Now, no matter what happened, I'd still have what I arrived at the ranch with, plus a pony.

One evening at the Manning's house, after supper had been cleared away and we three adults were sitting in the den with coffee watching Ashley play with some of Tommie's old toys, Lillian asked, "Joe, are you going to come through this lawsuit okay?"

"Sure, Lillian. Oh, I'll probably lose the ranch, and most of the money I have left will be gone, but I can handle that."

Fred looked at me with compassion. "Won't it hurt pretty bad to lose the ranch, Joe?"

I grinned at him. "Well, I'd be lying if I said it wouldn't, but since I lost Tommie the place doesn't have the good feeling it did. We had so many plans…" They both looked startled, and well they should. I guess it was the first time I'd spoken Tommie's name in front of anyone since her death.

"Fred, your daughter taught me a lot of things, but one lesson stands out from the rest. The most important things in life are unseen: love for and from family and friends, sitting in the middle of a good horse, breathing fresh country air, and laughing a lot. She was the sunshine in my life, and she showed me values that I had never seen before.

"Now, Tommie's gone, but she's left me with another ray of sunshine." I nodded toward the little blond head bent over a red fire engine. "As long as I have that little girl, the other things don't really matter."

I was not in court on the final day of the suit. As expected, the plaintiffs won, and the judge awarded them a judgment of ten million dollars. Because Howard Reagan didn't have any money, he was required to sell all of his equipment and turn over anything that was left to the court. I was assessed twenty-five percent of the damages or $2,500,000.00. Since I didn't have two and a half million dollars, I was required to sell my assets to raise what I could.

Jacob immediately appealed the decision, but he wasn't very hopeful that the appeal would be heard. There was just too much evidence against Reagan to expect the Court of Appeals to overturn the decision of the lower court.

Howard Reagan was also arrested for theft and forgery. I planned to go ahead with the charge so that Reagan wouldn't be free to dupe some other poor sucker, but I didn't really care much about it. There was no need for revenge in my makeup. Since my accountant and lawyer had all of the evidence against Reagan, they figured he would just plead guilty. So be it.

At first, Rita and Wendy took it hard that I was going to have to sell the ranch. The two wonderful women both suggested that they would work for nothing if it would help, but I just smiled and shook my head. "You can't know how much it means to me for you two ladies to offer, but I must refuse. As long as you work for me you will be paid. However, I'm afraid you should both begin looking for work elsewhere. Once this is over, I'm afraid I won't be able to afford any salaries, even if I had a house to keep you in."

The women wanted to be sad, but they both noticed that I was not unhappy at all. I went around whistling, and Ashley and I found a lot to laugh about. In some ways it felt good to be getting rid of the responsibility of having a lot of money and all the trappings that went with it. I found myself actually looking forward to being free again.

CHAPTER
TWENTY-SIX

Sale day came, and I made sure Rita took Ashley home with her. I didn't want my daughter to see things she was familiar with go to other people. I had already taken our personal things to the Manning's ranch early in the morning, and when the sale was final, I intended to pay off Roy and the other hands, pick up Ashley at Rita's, and go stay overnight with Fred and Lillian.

Since the front gate was left open, several reporters slipped in and tried to corner me for a statement. I had been news when I first won the lottery, and now that I was about to lose the money I was news again. With this in mind I had hired several security guards to keep an eye on things, and when one TV reporter became too obnoxious, I had the guards collect all of the news hounds up and take them to the gate.

The sale was not nearly as painful as I thought it might be. I hated to see Handy's Own, the fine mares and their foals go under the hammer, but they were bid in by a man who ran a quality horse ranch, so I knew they would have a good home. And the fine Angus cattle went to a local breeder that I knew, so I felt good about that.

By five o'clock the house and furniture had gone, the ranch was sold, and the sale was over. A representative of the court was there to accept the money for the judgment, a representative from the bank made an appearance to protect their part, and Harold Duckworth had come to keep both of the other two honest.

In the auction both my new pickup and Tommie's Expedition were sold, but I didn't much care. I was loading some personal items into Roy's pickup when Harold came up to me. "Joe, there was enough to settle the judgment, pay off the bank and all other bills, and you have almost a hundred thousand left. That includes your equity from the ranch. I have instructed the fellow from the bank to make out a cashier's check to you for the final amount. Is there anything else you need me for?"

"Harold, you have my thanks for being here today. I know you didn't have to come, and I appreciate it. The cashier's check is fine. I'm going to find another bank to do business with, so that will start a new account. Be sure to mail your invoice to the address I gave you, and you'll have my check in the mail. And of course, I'll want you to continue as my CPA."

The accountant shook his head. "I'm so sorry things worked out this way, Joe. You had to pay for the dishonesty of Howard Reagan, and that's just not right."

I grinned at him. "Well, at least I had the money to pay my part. Old Howard's going to jail for a long time for his sins, so I reckon I can't complain too much. "

"You're sure taking this well, Joe. Doesn't it make you mad?"

"It did at first," I replied, "but then I got to thinking about it, and this whole thing's been kind of unreal anyway. You know, I'm not really a rich rancher, Harold, I'm just a cowboy. Once I lost Tommie, this place didn't mean so much to me. And besides, I've got Ashley, and no amount of possessions could ever match what she's worth, so I reckon I'm ahead of the game."

Harold looked unconvinced, but then his world centered on money, and my casual attitude toward dollars was hard for him to understand. "So, what are you going to do now?"

"Well, I told you I'm just a cowboy, so I reckon I'll go see if I can find a job on a ranch somewhere."

We shook hands, and Duckworth went away shaking his head.

After everyone was paid off, Roy gave me a ride to the Manning's place, and pulled away with a tear in his eye. Roy and I had become close friends during the building up of the ranch, and I would sure miss him. I had called Matt and recommended Roy to him, so he had a job to go to, and Tom and Jose were going back to the Slash T also. The other two hands had found jobs already, so all the employees were taken care of.

Rita and Wendy brought Ashley out to the Manning ranch, and Ashley was so happy to see me, that her smile almost overcame Rita's tears. Wendy gave me a hug and went back to the car weeping, and Rita and I hugged for a long time. I thanked the wonderful woman that had taken such good care of me and my family, but I knew that no amount of thanks could ever really repay her.

Ashley and I stood in the driveway and waved as the two ladies drove away, and then we turned to the house where Fred and Lillian were waiting, singing *The Red River Valley* in loud voices as we stepped up on the porch.

CHAPTER TWENTY-SEVEN

In sudden relief from money and lawsuit pressures, we stayed with the Manning's for several days to just relax. I helped

Fred work some calves, and fix fence, and Ashley "helped" her grandmother with cooking and gardening. In the evenings we sat out on the patio or in the den, telling stories or listening as one of us read to Ashley. Tommie and I had agreed that we wanted our daughter to be a reader, we had actually started to read aloud to her when she was still in the womb, and it had worked; the little girl had been interested in books before she could talk. Now, at two-and-a-half, she would sit on my lap and turn the pages as I read a book to her. She knew the stories so well that she always turned the page at the right moment, even though she couldn't read the words yet. As I read, I taught her the alphabet by pointing to a letter and having her repeat it.

I noticed once when Lillian was listening she looked at Ashley, caught her breath, and a strange look came over her face. Later, she told me that Ashley's pretty profile was so much like Tommie's when she was a baby, that when she saw her granddaughter at that moment she was filled with emotion. We both got a little misty eyed when she told me.

One evening when I was brushing Ashley's fine blond hair, a nightly chore, Fred said, "Joe, you and Ashley have a home here for as long as you want. I'd forgotten how much fun it is to have a little one around."

I looked up and smiled at my father-in-law. "Thanks, Fred. I want Ashley to see as much of you folks as possible, and though I've got to look for work somewhere around, we'll always be no more than a day away." I gave my daughter a hug and continued, "But for now, young lady, it's time for bed."

Ashley wriggled off my knee and went to kiss her grandma goodnight, and then her grandpa, and off we went to the bathroom. When I had Ashley tucked in with prayers said, I came back to the den. "Fred, I'm going to start looking for work tomorrow, and I'll take Ashley along. Since fall is coming on, it's not the best time of year to look for a full time riding job, but maybe I'll get lucky. We may not be back tomorrow night, or for several days, but we will be back, and I'd like to leave Buck and Star here until I land something, if I can."

"Sure, son. You can leave your horses here as long as you want. And if you need some money, I can help out a bit."

I smiled and slowly shook my head. "Thanks, Fred. You're a real friend, but I don't need money. I came out of the mess I was in with about a hundred thousand, and Ashley's trust fund was protected, so I'm not in financial need. Still, in today's world $100,000.00 won't last forever, and I've proven that I can get rid of a *lot* of money in a short time. Mainly, I just need a job to feel like I'm doing something. Anyway, thanks for keeping the broomtails for me."

The next day was Monday, and Ashley and I waved good-bye about 8:00 and drove up the driveway. Ashley had asked only once about Rita and Wendy, and she was satisfied with my answer that they were still in Wichita Falls, and we'd see them one day soon. Because I had taken care of her almost from the moment she was born, to the little girl, I was the center of her universe. As long as Daddy was around, she was okay.

We spent the day down around Graham, Texas where I had grown up. I called at a few big ranches, but the answers to my inquiry about a job were all pretty much the same. They had all the full time help they needed, but there might be some part time work when fall roundup started. I was not disappointed, because I didn't really expect anything different.

By Wednesday we had been to all the ranches around Graham, and I pointed the pickup east along Highway 380. There were two towns on the highway that were shopping spots for the ranches around: one was Bryson, a small village about midway between Graham and the other town, Jacksboro, on east a few miles. South of Bryson there was a long, pretty valley with some fair sized places that I tried first, but there were no jobs to be had. By mid-afternoon, with Ashley asleep in her car seat, we headed toward Jacksboro.

The town of Jacksboro – originally named Jacksborough – began in the mid 1800's, and it had a violent history. At the end of the Civil War, because of Indian raids, Jacksboro was the Texas settlement furthest west in the state. In 1870 Fort Richardson was completed south of town. The fort was one of a string established by the U.S. Government to protect settlers from Indians, mostly Comanches. As the country became more settled, and the Indians were subdued and moved off to reservations in Indian Territory, some big ranches were established in Jack County.

I remembered when Ralph Richardson had come to my place and left with a check for $458,000.00. I knew that the ranch Ralph wanted to buy was north of Jacksboro, but I didn't have exact directions, and the map that Richardson had given me was in my deposit box at the bank in Wichita Falls.

I had received statements from the rancher each year after I made the loan, but I just sent them to my bookkeeper and hadn't paid much attention to them. The first one came when Tommie and I were falling in love, and I had been far more interested in the pretty girl in my life than in investments. Anyway, since I'd had so many other financial problems lately, I figured the money I'd loaned the rancher was gone now too, but I thought maybe Ralph Richardson would have a job opening, or know someone who did. It was worth a try at any rate. Now, if somebody could just tell me how to find the Bar M.

We checked into the Star Light Motel on the north edge of town, and settled in for the night. As I was putting Ashley to bed, she said, "You know, Daddy, I like to ride in the pickup, but do we have it do it every day?"

I kissed her on the forehead and replied, "Gets kind of tiresome, doesn't it honey? Tell you what, we've got one ranch to check on tomorrow, and then we'll go back to Grandpa and Grandma's. How's that sound?"

Eyes heavy with sleep, the little girl murmured, "Okay, Daddy."

The next morning I let Ashley sleep until she woke up by herself. I could see that a long day spent in a car seat was tiring for her, and I knew I had pushed a bit hard.

When I went to the office for coffee, I asked the clerk if he knew where the Bar M ranch was located, and not only did the man know about the ranch, but he gave me clear directions. The motel was at the junction of U.S. Highway 281 and State Highway 148, and I only had to go north on 148 until I crossed the West Fork of the Trinity River, and then turn west on the next county road.

By 10:00 a.m., Ashley had been fed and we were headed up 148. Just after crossing the infant Trinity River, I turned off on a gravel-covered county road and the dust began to boil up behind us. After about a mile, there was a sign that said "Bar M Ranch" in large black letters beside a ranch entrance. There were no other words, so I figured we were now on the Bar M.

By watching the odometer, I could see that we had traveled nearly ten miles after seeing the sign before the ranch buildings loomed ahead. It was late morning when I pulled into a large circle drive in front of a rambling brick-front ranch house. "I'm going up to the door there that you can see, Ashley. Will you be all right here in the truck?"

Ashley was eating corn chips out of a small bag, not exactly health food. She swallowed and said, "Sure, Daddy."

The large door had a knocker on the front made out of horseshoes, and a bell push to one side. I pushed the bell as being more polite than banging on the door, and after a few minutes the door was opened by a large woman wearing an apron. "Yes?" she inquired.

I pulled off my hat and said, "I'm looking for Ralph Richardson, ma'am."

"I'm sorry, but he's not here right now. He's gone to a cattle sale this morning, but he should be back this afternoon."

I thanked her, and turned away. I had taken two steps down the walk when the woman said, "His daughter's here if you'd like to talk to her."

I stopped and turned back. "Well, I'm lookin' for a job, so I reckon I should talk to Mr. Richardson. I'll come on back later today. Would you tell him Joe Garth stopped by?"

Turning again, I took two steps when I heard my named called by a different voice. "Joe! Joe Garth!" Once more I turned back to the house, and there stood *Lilly Walker*! I hadn't even thought about her for years, and yet there she was looking as pretty as ever, blond hair neatly arranged, brown eyes sparkling, and dimples showing.

"Lilly!" I shouted. "Where in the world did you come from?"

We met on the walk, and embraced as naturally as if we were old friends. "Ralph Richardson is my father," she said. "I'm taking a vacation, and I just love this place, though I grew up on the other ranch, so here I am. Now, why are you here?"

I told her about losing the ranch, and she already knew about Tommie dying. "I'm so sorry, Joe. I can see it still hurts."

I gave her a crooked smile, and then I shook my head and remembered Ashley. "Lilly, come on out to the truck with me. I want you to meet someone." We took the few steps to the old pickup, and I reached in the door and plucked Ashley out of her seat. "Ashley, say hello to a friend of mine, Lilly Walker."

"Hello, Lilly Walker," Ashley said, and then pushed her head into her my neck in sudden shyness.

"Oh, Joe," Lilly said. "She's beautiful."

"Shush," I replied. "I know she is, but I don't want her to get a big head."

Ashley giggled, for this was a game we often played. "My head's not big, Daddy. And you tell me I'm b'utiful all the time," she said in her grown-up voice. Lilly and I both laughed.

"Come on into the house, Joe and Ashley, and we'll have some lunch."

We had lunch and then we stayed into the afternoon, talking about everything. Ashley warmed to Lilly immediately and was soon sitting near her, and then in her lap. When it came time to take a nap, she wasn't happy until I let Lilly put her down. "I've never seen her take to anyone so quickly," I said.

"She's a lovely little girl Joe, and so unspoiled. How do you manage that when she's obviously the apple of your eye?"

"Well, I've had some help. Her grandparents live just outside Wichita, and they've been a lot of help. And then, before I sold the ranch, I had Rita and Wendy, two great ladies who ran the house and took care of Ashley when I was gone."

"Would that be the Rita I met when I came to interview you for the feature?"

"Why, yes, I'd forgotten that. Rita Blanco, a great cook and a good friend. She and her family were a lot of help to me when…" I stopped.

Lilly put her hand on top of mine and managed the awkward moment by saying, "I remember. You were looking for a cook and housekeeper, and you felt like Rita was the answer to your prayers."

We went on talking for a few minutes, and then we heard a man's voice from the kitchen asking Mrs. Huggins about something to eat. "There's Dad," Lilly said, and she got up and went into the kitchen, returning with Ralph Richardson.

"Joe Garth!" he exclaimed as he came into the room holding his hand out. I took the hand and shook it. "What brings you all the way down here to the sticks?"

"Ralph, it's good to see you. I'm hunting work, and I thought you might need a hand."

"Hunting work? Why, the last time I saw you there was money coming out of your ears. You gave me a check for nearly a half million dollars like it was an old newspaper. What happened?"

I grinned, liking the man's bluntness. "The oil business happened, Ralph."

Lilly got up and said, "I'll go check on Ashley while you two talk," and she left the room.

Ralph wanted to know how Lilly and I had met, and he explained that Lilly had taken her mother's maiden name, Walker, for professional reasons. He was proud of his daughter, and it showed, and I told him about Ashley and Tommie, and Ralph was real sorry to hear about Tommie's death. His wife, Lilly's mother, had died several years before so he really understood my pain.

Finally, we came back to my losing the money through

the wildcatter.

Ralph smiled. "Don't feel too bad, Joe. I got stung by that red wasp once myself. Cost me a lot of money and two years' calf crops to pull out. But there's something you should know. You don't have to find a riding job on another ranch, because you already own a part of the Bar M."

My mouth dropped open in amazement, and I shut it with a click. "Now, how could that be, Ralph?" I asked.

"Joe, you don't think I lost the money you loaned me, do you? When I bought this place, using some of my money and your $458,000.00, I knew it would be a good investment, I just didn't know how good. The estate wanted to sell, and in the deal we got three hundred and ten black-baldy mother cows, most with calves at side and bred back, and 42 Black Angus bulls. Also, we got half the oil and mineral rights, which is almost unheard of in this country. At the time of the sale, Texaco was drilling a well up near 148. The well came in two weeks after I took possession, and it's a good one. This place is a money maker."

A great load suddenly lifted off of my shoulders. Here was something I understood, a working ranch that was profitable, and I owned a share of it. "So, where do I fit in all of this, Ralph?"

"You originally owned fifteen percent of everything. As you instructed me, I've reinvested your share up to this point, so you now own 18%. Now, from what you've just told me, you want to work, so why not live right here and manage this ranch. I've still got my original place, and I really prefer to live there."

Around my huge grin, I said, "You've got a deal Ralph." We stood and shook hands, both knowing in range country ways that the handshake sealed the bargain.

We talked on about range conditions for a bit, and then I had a thought. "Ralph, does Mrs. Huggins go with this place?"

Ralph shook his head. "No, she doesn't. Mrs. Huggins is my housekeeper, and she runs the household staff at the Spring Ranch, my other place. She's only here because Lilly and I are staying a few days and she knows I can't do without her. You will have to get your own housekeeper."

I just smiled. I already knew who would soon be taking care of this place.

"Dad, this is Ashley," Lilly said from the doorway.

We turned and looked. Lilly was holding the still sleepy little girl, and Ashley smiled at us. When Lilly put her down, she went over to Ralph and said, "I'm pleased to meet you," in a grown up voice, and held out her hand.

Ralph squatted down in front of her and engulfed her tiny hand in his large one. "Howdy, Ashley," he said. "You know I don't have any grandchildren, would you like to be my grand-daughter?"

Ashley's face broke into a large smile. "You bet!" she replied, and gave him a big hug.

Later, after it was agreed that Ashley and I would spend the night, Mrs. Huggins called us in for supper, and with my first bite I could see why Ralph valued her.

CHAPTER TWENTY-EIGHT

On Monday, after a relaxing weekend on the Bar M, we returned to the Manning ranch, and I got on the phone. In no time I had Rita and Wendy agreeing to come back to work for us at the

Bar M, and in short order I loaded Buck and Star, waved to my in-laws, and Ashley and I were headed back to the ranch.

The foreman of the Bar M was a tall lanky cowboy with bright blue eyes and jet-black hair. His name was Michael O'Reilly, and his Irish ancestry was plain to see. When I returned to the ranch on that first Monday afternoon, I put Ashley down for her nap and went to the office where O'Reilly was waiting for me as arranged. We introduced ourselves and sat down. "Mr. Garth, Ralph called me last night and told me you'd be the manager here, and that I should come give you a report as soon as possible."

"Thanks for coming, Michael, and call me Joe. Sorry I wasn't here first thing this morning, but I had to wrap up a few things in Wichita County. Now, tell me how we stand for cows, and when you have the roundup planned."

We talked about the ranch, with Mickey, he preferred that to Michael or Mike, showing me on the map where the pastures were and how he planned to gather the cattle in each one. There were four large pastures fenced with five-strand barbed wire, and with good pipe-built working pens in each one. O'Reilly looked and talked like a cattleman, but I would reserve final judgment on his ability as foreman until I saw him at work with the men.

"When do you want to start the roundup?" Mickey asked.

"Well, if you have everything in place, why don't we start Thursday? Tomorrow I want to ride over the pastures with you and look at the pens, and Wednesday I'd like to talk to the men. Have you hired some extras for roundup?"

"Yep. We have seven full time hands here, and I usually hire an extra ten for roundup. We use some college boys from Tarleton U. at Stephenville mostly, and a couple of part time cowboys from Jacksboro. You want me to go ahead and contact them?"

"Do that, Mickey. Have them here by Wednesday afternoon, and I'll talk to all of them after supper."

Early the next morning Mickey picked up Ashley and me

to drive to the various pastures on the Bar M over rough country roads. Mickey drove a ranch pickup with four-wheel drive, and it was good that he did, for in several spots we needed the extra power to pull up out of deep gullies. After one really hard climb, I remarked, "Do we have a bulldozer on the ranch?"

"No, but there's a guy in town that hires out. We've used him a couple of times, and he does a good job."

"Well, this winter we'll get hold of him and see if we can do something about these roads."

The pastures still had plenty of grass left over from the good summer rains, and the cattle we saw were all in good shape. "How many mother cows are we running now, Mickey?" I asked.

"Just over five hundred. Ralph bought some extras last year, and we've raised up some real good heifers for next year. He figures this place will hold 600 to 700 cows in a good year, and we've had two of those. On the way back I'll show you the heifer pasture. We keep all the first-calf heifers in a hundred acre water trap near the headquarters in case they need help calving. One of us rides the trap every day. The ones who look close to calving we move to a pen closer in."

We got back to the house just after noon, and Ashley and I went into the house to see about lunch while Mickey headed for the cook shack at the bunkhouse. Ashley was kind of tired from the ride, and she dropped down on the couch for a rest while I made peanut butter and jelly sandwiches, my only claim to kitchen fame.

Before we could begin eating, a car horn sounded, and Ashley ran to the window to look out. "Aunt Rita! Aunt Wendy!" she shouted.

Sure enough, the two women were getting out of the car. I pulled the door open and we met them on the porch. "Welcome to the Bar M," I said, but it was hard to hear over Ashley's delighted yelps.

Once inside Rita immediately went to the kitchen and began working on a proper lunch while I helped Wendy haul the suitcases in. The house didn't really have servant quarters but there were several guesthouses linked to the main house by a covered enclosed walk. I gave the ladies their choice of these small comfortable buildings, and soon lunch was on the table.

It was good to have Rita and Wendy in residence, and I realized how much we had missed them. All the excitement had Ashley drooping before the meal was over, and Wendy took her off to her room for a nap.

With the two ladies in charge things would soon be running smoothly in the household, and I could devote my time to the cattle operation. I already loved the hills that surrounded the headquarters, and I suddenly realized how much I preferred the isolation of this ranch to the more-or-less exposed position of the Rafter JG.

Wednesday several pickups drove up to the parking area in front of the bunkhouse, and by suppertime all the temporary hands were gathered with the regular cowboys. Unlike the Slash T, the Bar M didn't hire ranch hands as such. Most of the ranch-hand work – fencing, haying, etc. – was contracted out, with some left for the full time cowboys to do in the winter.

I went down to the bunkhouse cook shack and ate with the men, and when the meal was over, and it was good, solid ranch food, and they were settled with cups of coffee, I stood up to speak to them. "I guess all of you know by now that I'm Joe Garth, and I'm the manager and part owner here. All of that looks good on the office stationary, but to you boys it's just blowing smoke unless I can handle my end of the job. Well, not long ago I was a working cowboy just like you.

"I rode for the Slash T out by Childress, and I had to earn my pay on the back of a horse. Then I struck it lucky and won the lottery. You probably all know about that, too. Of course, like you, when I get paid the first thing I want to do is spend all my money, and while it took me the best part of three years to do it, I've managed to get rid of that dough and now I'm back to working for a living." The men all laughed at this. It tickled them that I could go through several million dollars in such a short time and still laugh about it.

"I figure since I have to work again, this seems like a pretty good place to do it. We'll start roundup in the morning, and I'll be out there chasing cows with you, but I've moved up in the world a bit, so I don't have to sleep in here with all your dirty socks. I get to sleep in the Big House!" They all hooted at that and had wise comments to make. When they settled down, I finished. "Now, Mickey's the foreman and he'll have your orders for you. When it comes time to work the calves, I've got a mighty fine roping horse to use, so I won't have to be down in the dirt with the rest of you, but I'll be watching!" More laughter.

"Mickey, you can take over now. I'll leave so you can all cuss the boss in private."

As I walked away from the bunkhouse I could still hear their laughter. Always leave them laughing, I thought.

We didn't see Lilly again for a couple of weeks. I worked from early to late at the roundup, and Ralph came over to lend a hand, along with a couple of his home-ranch boys. The work was hard but rewarding as calves were branded, castrated and vaccinated, cows were doctored, and yearlings were separated for shipping. I soon saw that Mickey was a fine foreman, not too good to get his hands dirty, but also on top of the head count and supervision of the hands.

When we worked the pastures close to headquarters, I would take Ashley with me for part of the day, riding Star. I watched her so she didn't get into any trouble, but the little girl was a natural horsewoman, so I didn't worry much. Of course, Rita and Wendy thought she was way too little to be riding a horse, but I just smiled at their fears and took her anyway.

During those hard weeks Lilly did call several times to see how we were settling in. Ashley talked to her sometimes on the phone, and she was always smiling when the call was over. I was pleased to hear from Lilly, and I suggested that she come for the weekend after we finished the roundup. "And before you take that in the wrong way, Wendy, Ashley's great nanny, will be here as chaperone. Rita goes home to her family on weekends, but Wendy prefers to stay here and have two days off during the week, so you won't have to worry about me making a pass at you." I laughed, and Lilly laughed with me.

"Better look out, Joe. You're a very eligible bachelor, you know. *I* might be the one making a pass."

When I rang off, I told Ashley that Lilly would be coming to see us on Saturday. Her face lit up and she immediately began to bounce up and down singing, "Lilly's coming! Lilly's coming!" and then she ran out of the room to tell Rita.

Watching her, Wendy said, "I guess you can take that as approval, Joe. Who's Lilly?"

I told her, and then left the room. As I went out the door I saw Wendy headed for the kitchen, and I figured she and Rita would have their heads together trying to match-make. They could try all they wanted, but I wasn't ready for that yet, so they had their work cut out for them.

On Saturday morning I was up even earlier than usual. I went out first thing to check on a pen of ten heifers that were due to calve soon, and then I came back to the house. Wendy didn't cook as lavishly as Rita did, but on weekends she would do the basics. When I got back to the house, she was in the kitchen, and I could smell sausage frying.

"Mornin', Wendy,"

"Good morning, Mister Joe. You must have gotten up way before the birds this morning."

"Yes, I did. Woke up early and couldn't seem to go back to sleep," I replied as I poured both of us a cup of coffee. Wendy smiled as if she might just know why I couldn't sleep, but I ignored her.

We were just sitting down to breakfast when a small blond head appeared looking around the kitchen door. "Is Lilly here yet?" Ashley asked.

I smiled at her as she climbed up on my lap and snuggled back against me, still sleepy. "No, babe, not yet. It's still real early, and why are *you* up before the chickens?"

Children have no need to pretend about their feelings. "I just woke right up thinking about Lilly. I really like her, and I want her to come soon."

At 9:00 a.m., when Lilly pulled up before the house, Ashley and I were seated on a bench on the front porch watching for her. She got out of her car as we came down the walk. "What a nice welcoming committee," she said, and Ashley ran the last few feet to jump into her arms

I grinned and took her hand, and then leaned forward and kissed her on the cheek. Lilly squeezed my hand. "And you told me I'd be safe," she said with a smile.

It was a beautiful early October day, and we spent most of it outside, driving and walking over the ranch, or sitting on the patio and talking. The evening was just cool enough to light a fire in the huge stone fireplace, and after a nice dinner, the three of us settled down in the den with Ashley on Lilly's lap. Lilly sighed deeply. "You know, when I graduated high school in Jacksboro, I couldn't wait to get away. Living on a ranch in the country seemed so un-cool. And when I went to the University of Texas in Austin, I just knew I was a big city girl captured in a country girl's body, but a funny thing happened to me about midway through my freshman year. I suddenly wanted to come home."

"You mean you quit school?" I asked.

"No, I didn't quit, but I began to come home on weekends to see Mom and Dad, and I would saddle my horse, and just ride over the ranch, something I hadn't done for years. Then, on Sunday night I would go back to Austin and try to recapture the excitement of living in a big city, but it never seemed the same."

"And I suppose you brought some of those city boys from college home from time to time; what did they think of the ranch?"

Lilly laughed. "Not much, I can tell you. Most of them couldn't wait to get back to Austin." She grew serious. "Do you remember the last time you called me, Joe, after we had dinner at Uncle Lynn's?"

"Sure do. Some guy answered, and I figured he was your boyfriend, so I didn't call again."

"That's what I thought. Well, that was one of those college boys from Austin. I dated him quite a lot when we were in school together, and I'd gone down to Austin to see him a time or two after I graduated, but I could see we would never really have anything. He hated the country, and he only came up to Wichita Falls, which he called a 'hick town', to try to get me to come back to Austin and live with him.

"I was furious when he answered the phone. He had no right to do that, he just grabbed it and said hello. And after you hung up I just knew I'd never hear from you again. It made me so mad I sent that boy packing, and I haven't heard from him since. I called one other time, but you didn't invite me out, so I figured that was very much that."

I thought for a minute, looking at this pretty girl holding my daughter on her lap. "So, any boyfriends around now?"

"No, and I think I'm glad about that."

"And, do you like living in Wichita Falls? That 'hick town' still seems like a big city to me."

"Well, it's sure bigger than Jacksboro!" Lilly said with a laugh. "When I graduated college I had to have a job, and I had a degree in journalism, so I went to Wichita and applied at the newspaper, and I got a job. But Dad will tell you I come home about two weekends a month. There's just something about the country that I can't seem to do without."

"Do you still ride when you come home?"

"Oh, yes. My horse Sonny is a buckskin like yours, only lighter. He's getting old now, but he still likes to go, so we get along real well."

"How about taking a ride tomorrow? We could go get your horse at Spring Ranch and ride here. Ashley has a pony, and Buck needs some exercise."

Lilly's face lit up. "Oh, yes! That would be great."

"Okay, it's settled. And, uh, Lilly, Ashley and I go to church on Sunday's at First Methodist in Jacksboro. You're welcome to come with us, or stay at home, whichever you choose. We go to the early service because I like contemporary music, and we also like to have an early lunch at the Green Frog Café right after Sunday school."

"Joe! I've been a member of First Methodist since I was twelve! Of course I want to go with you. What time do I have to be ready?"

The next morning I opened the door of the church, and Lilly passed through ahead of me holding Ashley's hand. Some heads turned, and Lilly greeted old friends, and when we entered the sanctuary, it felt very natural to be sitting in a pew with Ashley between us, and I wondered about that.

Later we went to the Green Frog for Sunday dinner. I had a trailer hooked to the pickup, and after Sunday dinner, we went to Ralph's home ranch and picked up Lilly's horse. By the time we returned to the Bar M, Ashley was ready for her nap, and while she slept, Lilly and I talked and walked around the ranch buildings.

"Think you'll ever remarry, Joe?" Lilly asked.

I was quiet for a minute. We had stopped to look at the heifers, and I leaned on the fence, hooking one boot heel over the bottom rail. "Yes, I reckon I will. I liked being married, and I know Ashley needs a woman in her life. I was thinking the other day about when she's a teenager, *and I don't want that to happen in a hurry*! There's no way I can help her with a lot of female things then. Yes, I reckon I'll marry again when the right girl comes along. How about you?"

"Oh, I've always wanted to be married, but I haven't met many men that I'd want to have around all the time. I guess I'm like you, when the right man comes along..."

Lilly smiled gently. "You know, last night I woke up when a little girl crawled into my bed. She snuggled up against me and said, 'You sure are warm and soft, Aunt Lilly,' and then she went to sleep."

"The little minx. She does that to me once in a while, and

I've let her get away with it. Sorry if she disturbed you."

Lilly laughed. "Oh, no, Joe, she didn't disturb me at all. I was really flattered, and I loved having her with me. I've never been around children that much, but if they're all like Ashley, I'd like to change that. It made me think that I might like one of my own some day."

Sunday was as pretty as Saturday had been, and when Ashley woke up we all enjoyed our afternoon ride.

I held Ashley in my arms and we both waved at Lilly as she drove down the driveway just at dusk.

"Daddy?" Ashley said, "Will Lilly be coming back?"

"Yep. She'll be here next Friday night. You like her don't you?"

"Oh, yes! I think she likes me, too!"

"I'll bet you're right. What were you two whispering about just before Lilly left?"

"Oh, just girl things," Ashley replied in a grownup voice. "She said I should take good care of you until she comes back, and I said I would. I'd sure like to have Lilly here all the time, wouldn't you, Daddy?"

We started back up the walk, and I sat down on the bench by the front door, pulling Ashley up on my lap. "Well, I wouldn't mind."

"Is Lilly going to be my new mama?" Ashley asked in the direct way of all children.

I kissed the top of her head and replied, "I don't know yet, baby, but we'll see."

As I carried the little girl back to the house, I heard her whisper to herself, "I hope so."

Would it be possible for me to love someone again as I had loved Tommie? Probably not, but then everything would be different. I had to admit that I felt love growing for Lilly, and I sure remembered the symptoms. And I kind of thought she felt the same way about me. I knew I needed a woman to share my life, and as much as I tried to be both parents to Ashley, I also knew that she needed a mother. I'd watched as she and Lilly began a relationship, and there was something going on that had to do with females that I really didn't understand, but I enjoyed it anyway.

Later, when Ashley was in bed, the phone rang. "Hi, Joe. Just thought I'd call to say thanks for a great weekend. I've got to tell you, your little girl has won my heart."

"I think you've won hers, too, Lilly. She told me when I was reading her a story tonight that she hoped you would be back to tuck her in real soon. Her daddy's tucking in is okay, but Lilly's is better."

Lilly laughed, a sound I was coming to enjoy. "I'll see you Friday night, Joe. And tell Ashley that I love her."

"I will. Thanks for calling, Lilly." We hung up, and I sat looking into the fire for a bit. Then I whispered to myself, "Could there be another one? Maybe, just maybe....."

The End

Other Books by Herb Marlow

www.herbmarlowbooks.com

Modern War
In Harm's Way
Gunner Hobbs
Island Song
The Fools Brigade

Civil War
Winchester Doctor

Contemporary Christian Series
Ministerwanted.com
Minister Wanted: Santa Fe
Minister Wanted: Wichita Falls
Minister Wanted: Portland, Oregon

Western Old West
South Texas Mean
Outlaws West

Jericho Shade Series
Jericho Shade
Texas Comes Calling
Johnny's Run
Shade Mountain Ranch

The River Series
Trouble on the Bosque
Drive the Pecos
Red River Rising

Contemporary Western
Cowboy Riches
Mesquite Riches

Western Short Story Collections

Wild Horse & High Mountains
Hot Texas Morning
Dangerous Ground
High Lonesome
Cowboys and Widows

Contemporary Novels
The Going Away
To Everything a Season
Hood River Home
Cowboy Riches
Mesquite Riches

Contemporary Short Story Collection
On the Edge of Spring

Children's Books
Ghost Horse
Cougar!
Sundancer
Jack the Border Collie

Non-Fiction
Write Your Book – Now!
A Students Guide to Successful Writing
Time Out for Teachers
The Classroom Story Teller

The Parenting Series
Her First Word Was – No!
I don't Know – I didn't do it!
Always Phone First